BEST GAY
ROMANCE
2009

BEST GAY ROMANCE 2009

EDITED BY
RICHARD LABONTÉ

Published in the United States.
Cleis Press Inc., P.O. Box 14697, San Francisco, California 94114.

Printed in the United States.
Cover design: Scott Idleman
Cover photograph: Queerstock
Text design: Frank Wiedemann
Cleis logo art: Juana Alicia
First Edition.
10 9 8 7 6 5 4 3 2 1

For Asa, forever the Best Romance

Contents

| INTRODUCTION

I t was a surprise to me that there weren't any—any!—stories about marriage among the submissions for *Best Gay Romance* this year. Gay weddings can be pretty romantic, right? But queers don't really need a license for certifying love. Just each other. As it should be.

That said, I'm a romantic.

And despite my disdain for licenses, a married one—Asa and I (he's the fellow to whom this and other Cleis collections I've edited are dedicated) were wed as much out of practicality as desire. That was in 2003, ten years after we met in San Francisco; our marriage made his quest for permanent Canadian residency much easier. The wedding party was fun; fifty friends had a great time eating and drinking and dancing. Asa's mother was there from Nashville. Two friends who'd never met hooked up for the night. My gay world intersected with my straight world. A good time was had.

But we did it for that license.

Back to being a romantic.

I've read many thousands of gay erotic short stories over the years, in the course of editing assorted anthologies about bondage and bears and boys in heat, and for the *Best Gay Erotica* series, now fourteen years old—almost legal (in some jurisdictions)! And it's certainly fun to read porn (mostly literary porn, so-called "literotica," but still...), stories about the myriad ways two men can be sexual, from passionate lovemaking to downright kinky behavior.

But give me some wry sweetness, some wistful memories, some settled domesticity, some happy-ever-after, even some sad endings, and I'm a puddle of queer contentment.

You'll find all of those qualities, wry and settled, sweet and wistful, sad and happy, in these stories about men meeting men and men loving men and men surviving the loss of men. And not a single wedding...

Richard Labonté
Bowen Island, BC

ONE

T. Hitman

Lyle was already feeling like a pariah when Mike leaned over him to grab another stack of corrugated boxes off the shelf. He tried his best not to gawk or react, difficult feats to pull off given the closeness of the other man's bare legs, so solid and furry; the hypnotic scent of him, a trace of fresh, masculine sweat mixed with the deodorant Mike had slapped on earlier that morning; the meaty fullness packed into the front of his camouflage cutoffs—all tempting Lyle to steal a glance.

The atmosphere in the warehouse was tense enough and growing worse with every day that passed since Kevin Collins had pointed out the bear paw-print sticker on the back bumper of Lyle's truck. It wasn't a rainbow flag, but it hadn't taken much after that to polarize the men. Even Mike had been less of a buddy in recent weeks. The handsome, late-thirtysomething go-to guy that Lyle had fallen in crush with on Day One had gotten colder and quieter since Collins spilled the news about what the sticker meant to the rest of the warehouse crew.

"Help me a sec?" Mike's deep, powerful voice shattered the spell Lyle had fallen under—but not the temptation to look, to draw in a deep breath of the Mike-flavored air, thus taking at least a part of the other man inside him. Penetration by proxy, Lyle thought.

"Sure."

Together they lugged two more stacks of unassembled corrugated cardboard boxes onto the pallet, filling the first of the morning's orders.

Unable to resist, Lyle let his eyes wander for a few dangerous seconds, just enough time to drink in Mike's unrivaled magnificence. His dark hair, in a neat athlete's haircut, was going silver around the edges, right above his ears. An old T-shirt bearing the logo of the local pro baseball team showcased the muscles of his chest and arms to perfection, the pits damp with sweat, the collar near his throat prickly with a thatch of dark hair that trailed up into the days-old scruff coating the lower half of his handsome face.

Mike's ass was high and square, a leftover from his years in the army that he'd maintained by playing all of the Big Four sports—baseball in the summer, ice hockey in the winter, pigskin and hoops in the seasons between. His old construction boots flashed a hint of clean white sock at the top. When you factored in Mike's blue eyes, which looked wounded even when he smiled, the dimple on his right cheek, and his no-bullshit, easygoing blue-collar work ethic, the end result was almost blinding to behold.

And impossible to ignore.

Lyle picked up the work order. "Anything else I can help you with?"

"Nope," Mike said.

Lyle forced himself to look away as the other man grabbed

the pallet jack's hydraulic handle and gave it a few firm pumps, ignoring the ache in his stomach signaling that Kevin Collins and the other straight, intolerant yahoos who toiled in the aisles of the cavernous State Street Warehouse had turned Mike against him. He was alone now. One.

Despite the endless succession of jerk-off fantasies that had sustained Lyle over the past few months, he had no illusions about the truth of the situation. He was twenty-eight, living by himself in a one-bedroom apartment a few miles and a pair of right turns up the road from State Street. Mike was straight, ten years older, a lone wolf if the snippets and sound bites Lyle had collected turned out to be true. Wasn't married, but most likely kept at least one if not a bunch of lady friends at the ready, because he was a man and men had needs.

Lyle understood a man's needs better than he gave himself credit for.

That afternoon, about an hour before the jarring buzzer would sound, releasing them all from what sometimes felt like modern-day slavery, Lyle spotted Mike standing alone on the loading dock, leaning against the wall, one giant foot crossed over the other. He was staring off into space, his blue eyes—bluer than even the sky—oblivious to Lyle's presence.

The knot in Lyle's stomach pulled tighter. He wanted to march over, to ask Mike how he was doing, was everything all right between them, any chance he could explain his side of what Kevin had turned into the biggest scandal to hit State Street Warehouse since the previous year's Christmas party, which was still spoken about occasionally during lunch breaks by the other knuckle draggers. But his sneakers wouldn't obey his heart, and he kept right on walking.

The next day, Mike didn't show up for work. Nor did he the

day after that. By Friday, Lyle was feeling isolated and shunned by the rest of the warehouse. The last of his kind.

"Hey, Kevin," Lyle said.

The other man took a step back, coughed to clear his throat, and said, "Not so close. I don't want to get what you have. What up, homo?"

Lyle gaped, " 'Scuse me?"

"Homes. What up, *homes*?"

Lyle let it slide. The under-the-breath comments, snickers, and stares had gotten too obvious to blame on simple paranoia. Lyle didn't eat lunch with the rest of the warehouse workers any more, and rarely spoke to any of them, except on an as-needed basis. Even approaching Kevin to ask about Mike had taken more effort than not allowing his gaze to linger too long on his hunky supervisor, before Mike had gone missing.

"Have to ask you something."

"What about—sports? Pussy?"

Lyle ignored the snark. "Mike—where the hell is Mike?"

"Big Mike?" Kevin parroted. "He didn't tell you?" Lyle shrugged. "Hate to be the one to break the news, seeing as how much guys like you love another man's balls. Mike had to have one of his lopped off. Cancer, dude. Bet that ruins your day almost as much as his."

Kevin walked away, leaving Lyle frozen where he stood. From the corner of his eye, Lyle saw the other man yank the leg of his loose-fit shorts up. He turned in time to see Kevin's balls spill into the open. Kevin wagged his hairy sac at him, chuckled, and continued on his way.

The rest of the afternoon passed in a blur. Lyle felt numb, going through the motions, only partially aware of time and space. The few times he tried to press his coworkers for more information, he was met with apathy and condescension. Mike's boss told Lyle he couldn't discuss the situation due to medical privacy laws.

With no other option, Lyle consulted a reliable fallback: the telephone book in the junk drawer in his kitchen.

Heart galloping, he approached the apartment block's front door. The building was an ugly, square, brick throwback to the 1970s with zero personality. The kind of place that unleashed a feeling of despair in Lyle whenever he saw one, a place where hopelessness was a tenant. Not fitting for the caliber of a man like Mike.

For days, Lyle had picked up the phone only to hang it up again before dialing past the first few numbers. Driving to the place, parking his truck with its bear-paw bumper sticker in the spot right next to Mike's rugged SUV, Lyle felt like a stalker. He almost backed out and drove away, but killed the ignition and pocketed the keys before he chickened out.

There was no denying the fact that Lyle was attracted to Mike. That mysterious chemical spark had flared the moment they'd first shaken hands in the warehouse. Hell, he hadn't pumped his cock thinking about anyone else for months, hadn't slept with another warm body for much longer than that, was sustained only by his fantasies because contrary to what Kevin and the others thought, Lyle wasn't the kind of guy who slept with a different dude every night. He was a romantic at heart—and his heart had been captured by one man and one man only, Mike Logan.

Sometimes, Lyle would do a crazy trick he'd performed when he was younger: lay in bed with his spine braced against the headboard and his legs over his head, jerking his dick until he shot into his open and hungry mouth. In those moments, he pretended the juice was Mike's as he devoured it, jealous and envious of every mouth that had tasted the legit thing in the real world.

But as much as he lusted after Mike's body, he also really liked Mike, the human being. And being a good friend meant helping a person out when he was down, even if he hadn't asked for it.

Lyle grabbed the bag containing a six-pack and a package of cookies off the passenger seat and tromped up the brick stairs to the door, his heart pounding in his chest. He found the right apartment and buzzed, then waited. After several interminably long seconds, the squawk box squawked.

"Yeah?"

"Hey, Mike," Lyle said, his already-dry mouth draining of the last of its spit. "It's Lyle. From work."

He added the last part in haste—quantifying his identity spared him from how he knew it would feel if Mike asked *Who?* Then he thought, *How many Lyles can the man know?*

The intercom died. The squeak of a door's hinges from somewhere deep in the apartment building's dark interior sounded, alerting Lyle to a flash of motion from beyond the security door's glass. Mike. He appeared and opened the door.

"Hey, man," Lyle said, smiling widely.

"Dude," Mike greeted him, indifferent.

It took the greatest effort not to stare at Mike's clean white T-shirt, blue jeans, and bare feet. Lyle did, however, notice that Mike's puppy-dog eyes looked even more wounded than usual.

"Hope you don't mind me dropping in like this."

"Why are you here?" Mike growled.

Lyle shrugged. "Thought you could use a friendly face. The baseball game's coming on, and I brought beer."

Mike smiled, but the gesture contained little humor. "You know?"

Lyle nodded.

"I'm off the beer for a while."

"I also brought cookies."

Mike drew in a deep breath, his annoyance—hell, his anger—obvious, barely contained. But just when Lyle figured he'd made a mistake in coming here, Mike's furry mouth curled into a smile that was more convincing than its predecessor. "What kind of cookies?"

"Chocolate chip. The soft, squishy kind, from the bakery," Lyle said. "Only the best for you, man."

The apartment was a typical bachelor's cave, with mismatched furniture. A soft and overstuffed chair in front of a widescreen TV hooked up to the usual gadgets and games, a baseball poster tacked to one wall beside it. Mike's familiar work boots sat just inside the door, a discarded pair of sweat socks bunched inside them. Several pill bottles littered the top of the kitchen table, along with stacks of unopened mail and a stroke magazine.

"So how are you doing, big Mike?" Lyle said, drawing in a deep breath of the Mike-scented air.

"How do you think?"

Lyle shrugged. "Probably not too good."

"No, probably not," Mike said.

Lyle set the bag down on the counter and pulled out the cookies. "I wanted to bring you something, but I didn't peg you as the flower or fruit basket type."

Mike snorted, slumped into his big chair, and thumbed the remote. Lyle tossed the beer into the fridge, which was populated by a threadbare collection of protein shakes, yogurt, and bottles of sports drinks. He picked up the cookies but wasn't in the mood to eat them any more than Mike seemed to be.

"So when are you coming back to work?"

"Don't know. Depends on how I feel. Next week, maybe."

"Good, because it isn't the same there without you."

Mike sighed, flipped through channels to the pregame show, then continued on through the dial. The air in the apartment, except for the hollow cadence of channels flying past on the TV screen, fell oppressively silent. At the periphery of Lyle's line of sight, he glimpsed thick black leg hair poking out of the cuffs of denim, right above Mike's ankles, and the undeniable sexiness of the other man's enormous bare feet. If he forced his eyes to roam higher, he'd easily be able to track his way up to Mike's crotch. Lyle desperately wanted to look but couldn't make himself do it. It grew harder by the second to breathe.

"Kevin Collins still being a dickhead to you?" Mike asked, bringing Lyle out of his trance.

"Huh?"

"I warned him, last day I was on the job. Told him to cut the shit or I'd show him some serious harassment."

Lyle waved a hand to dismiss it. "He is, as you've said, a dickhead. But don't worry about it. You've got bigger things on your plate."

"He *has* been harassing you? Fuckin' asshole," Mike sighed. "I know about you. About what, you know, you're into."

Lyle choked down a heavy swallow. The words he planned to offer in his defense died somewhere in his throat.

"You got a guy?"

Lyle shook his head. "You got a girl?"

"Naw," Mike said. "I haven't gotten laid since...shit, like a hundred years before the surgery. Don't even know if I can still perform."

"Course you can," Lyle said. "Can't you?"

"Not exactly been in the mood. Haven't felt much like trying, being as I'm half the man I used to be."

"Are you kidding? Look at that dude Lance Armstrong. Losing a nut didn't stop him from being a stud. That handsome fucker was screwing the hottest chick in rock and roll for a while."

Mike shrugged. "I appreciate you saying that, but I'm not much of a stud anymore."

"Oh, man," Lyle chuckled. "Lance ain't got nothing on you...."

Eyes narrowed, Mike said, "Shut the fuck up."

"Seriously, you're the whole package."

"Bad choice of words," Mike said, pointing at his crotch.

"Heart, soul—and with a super-sized dose of handsome thrown in."

Mike's face went red as he broke their gaze, but his smile persisted. "But with half the balls."

"There's more to a man's being sexy than whether he has two balls or one," Lyle said. "Case in point, Kevin thought he was being funny the other day when he wagged his raisin-nuts at me in the warehouse."

Anger flashed across Mike's face. "He did *what*?"

"Trust me when I tell you, the joke was on him. Kevin may have both his balls, but he's nowhere the man you are," Lyle continued. He realized that he'd started to ramble, but now that it was all out on the table, he couldn't stop himself, and probably wouldn't have if given the choice. "If you're asking, I'll tell you. Tell you why. For starters, those puppy-dog eyes of yours. How you don't shave for a couple of days, and you get all that scruff. It's so sexy."

"It's *lazy*."

"It makes you look like a pirate, a palooka," Lyle said. "And when it's a hundred fuckin' degrees in that warehouse and your arms are dripping with sweat, you still look like a million bucks. Those hairy legs of yours...fuck, even your big feet."

"My feet?" Mike snorted again.

"Yeah, in those old work boots. It drives me crazy to see you strutting around in them, especially when you wear your camouflage cutoffs. Makes your butt insanely hot. And, of course, your bulge. So you got one nut less now, big deal. I bet your one is still fatter than most other dudes' two."

The knowledge that he was blathering and had crossed the line finally struck Lyle.

"Shit, I'm sorry, man. I shouldn't have said all that."

Lyle stood. He started for the door, but Mike's voice stopped him from retreating.

"Wait," Mike said.

Lyle hit the brakes and revolved.

"Since this happened, you're the only guy from work who's made the effort to ask how I'm doing. Thanks for saying it, for making me feel good about myself."

"Any time," Lyle said. "I think you're a hell of a guy."

"My feet," Mike repeated, lifting up one of his giants and examining it. "You think they're sexy?"

"Oh, very much so," Lyle said. "Most men don't know it, but their feet are their most underrated sex organs."

Lyle couldn't believe what happened next, any more than Mike seemed able to comprehend just how incredible the unthinkable idea could feel. With the baseball game droning on low in the background, Lyle sat Indian-style between Mike's legs. Mike reclined in his big chair, offering his feet, one at a time, into Lyle's hands.

"*Dude...*" Mike moaned.

Lyle applied gentle but firm pressure and massaged Mike's naked foot from ankle to instep, sole to topside, eventually reaching toes. Starting with the small one, Lyle rubbed them in order, all the way to the big toe.

Mike shifted in his seat and groaned, signs that Lyle at first assumed were due to the other man's discomfort.

"Want me to stop?"

"Hell, no," Mike sighed, closing his eyes. His hairy throat knotted with a difficult swallow, something not lost on Lyle. As aware of Mike as he was, Lyle didn't realize his cock had gotten stiff until he shifted to accommodate the man's other foot.

"You're sure?"

"Feels great, pal," Mike said, his voice barely above a whisper.

Lyle drew in a deep breath. "I can make it feel even better…if you want."

Eyes still closed, Mike nodded.

Lyle raised Mike's foot to his mouth and began to suckle his big toe, as though it were a smaller version of his cock.

"Fuck," Mike growled. "Aw, fuck…"

Lyle continued nursing on Mike's toes, but worried he'd gone too far, that the realization of the line they'd crossed would hit fully home to Mike, sending a man who had already been sorely tested by life in recent weeks into a blind rage.

"*Fuck*," Mike repeated.

Lyle glanced up to see Mike's eyes were open, as if telegraphing that he had, indeed, come out of his trance, had landed hard and found another dude touching and tasting him in a way most straight men would find unthinkable.

Lyle spit the toe out of his mouth. "Mike?"

"I don't fuckin' believe it. Dude…"

For several tense seconds, Lyle was sure Mike was going to deck him. But then Mike snaked both hands down to his crotch and hastily unzipped his blue jeans. He fished out his dick and let it hang in clear view, gloriously hard.

"I haven't gotten a boner since this whole fuckin' nightmare started," Mike said, a wide smile breaking across his handsome face. "Not since...fuck...thanks, man."

Mike eased his foot away from Lyle's mouth and leaned forward, cupping his cheeks in both powerful hands. A mix of relief and giddy excitement flooded Lyle's insides.

"I told you there were other parts of your body more important, you know, than balls," Lyle said, smiling back.

For a moment, he wondered if Mike, overwhelmed by excitement, might actually kiss him, crush their mouths together, perhaps wrangle Lyle's tongue into submission with his. The look in Mike's eyes said all that his lips could not, that Lyle had pulled him back from the dead, had saved him body and soul, and that Lyle had given him a better gift than any woman—any *person*—ever had.

"So how about you help me out with this part, now," Mike growled, releasing Lyle's face and giving his cock a shake.

By the time Mike returned to the job, Lyle had revealed other secrets about his body Mike hadn't considered before the surgery, that toes and earlobes, throat and armpits, legs and asshole could also give a man an amazing erection thanks to the licks of another male's tongue, if he simply opened himself up to the possibilities of finding love in unexpected places.

Lyle didn't see Kevin's elbow coming at him. Lightning quick, the powerful jab collided with his shoulder, knocking him into the nearby shelf.

"Sorry," Kevin said. It was obvious by the chuckle he added that he really wasn't.

Lyle straightened. Less than a minute later, Kevin was on his knees in front of him, held in place by a powerful armlock.

"Apologize," Mike ordered.

"Let go of me, fucker!"

"Oh, dude, I'm *this close* to letting you go—right out the fuckin' door, unless you make good with your esteemed coworker and cut the shit."

"I was just joking around," Kevin pleaded.

"Nobody's laughing. This guy you've been fucking with has more balls than you, me, and the rest of the warehouse combined. I see or hear one more deliberate attack against him, I'll clean house. You and your pals got that straight?"

"Yeah," Kevin muttered, surrendering. "I'm sorry."

Mike released him. "Now prove it. Get the fuck back to work!"

Kevin grumbled a blue streak of curses under his breath, but none of them were directed against Lyle.

"You okay, pal?" Mike asked.

Lyle rubbed his shoulder. "Sure am."

Mike nodded and turned to go, but then pivoted back in Lyle's direction. "You up for hanging out tonight?"

"Always."

"Game's on, and maybe you could stay over. You know…"

"Love to," Lyle said.

As he turned to continue filling the order he'd been picking when Kevin side-armed him, Mike gave Lyle's butt a friendly pat. Lyle cast a look at the prominent bulge in Mike's camouflage pants, no longer afraid of stealing glances because permission had been granted.

The ones had become two.

COMING BACK TO ME

Simon Sheppard

know: wish fulfillment. But sometimes wishes come true, and not only at Disneyland.

God, how I've loved him. Love him still. At the risk of seeming overly sentimental. I'll take that risk. Yes, we met unromantically, at a fairly wild party at the mostly gay commune down the street, where I spotted him getting blown in a corner. He was stoned and I was stoned and when the guy who was sucking him got off his knees, I was impressed with Charlie's...attributes. So I went over to him and something...happened. Just happened, rich and strong. But like I said, we were both very stoned.

After that night, we began seeing each other, me sneaking visits to his attic room, sticky in the heat of an Ohio summer. Since it wasn't just any summer, but the summer of 1967, we spent a whole lot of our time together stoned, planning our getaway to San Francisco. Because, let's face it, it was a whole lot harder to be a good hippie in some Hicksville college town in the middle of the country than in the Haight or the East Village.

It was harder to be a homo, too, though that didn't stop us from spending plenty of time together, mostly naked.

Neither of us had dropped acid before, and we decided to give it a shot the night of a Jefferson Airplane concert. It was amazing, of course, though if we hadn't been with friends, we probably never would have gotten home. I mean, we'd still be there, our sweaty tie-dyed T-shirts stuck to our skinny-but-cosmic bodies. And yes, there were some rough patches, as with—I was subsequently to find out—any trip, but then Charlie smiled a cosmic smile, both innocent and knowing, fuzzy-eyed, and it was all right. By the end of the night he and I were wrapped in each other's arms. And I mean wrapped. And the first time he came inside me, I felt that the universe itself exploded into shards of shimmering light. It was like a Grateful Dead jam. Only better.

Summer turned to fall, as summers will, I guess, and then to a bitter-cold winter. Dreams of San Francisco receded, dreams of love didn't. Everybody talks about the crazy wonderfulness of first love, and in our case, that was totally accurate. I was in my last year of college, he was working at some lousy job packaging essential oils and handmade soaps, we were head over heels in love. We explored each other's bodies and souls, swore undying devotion. Charlie got free incense at work. What more could one ask from life?

Except that I wanted more. I hated to admit it. It was so... ego-driven. And, as we'd both learned on our voyages through chemical nirvana, ego was an illusion and a trap. But I wanted to be somebody. With him (preferably) or without him. I wanted to go to New York and be an artist. Or an actor. Or a filmmaker. Something. Something famous, successful.

See, another thing about first love affairs is that they tend to be confused. Most people, lacking experience in the weirdness of love, just can't navigate the shoals. Yes, I was amazed that someone—anyone—could love me the way he said he did. And yes, he was the world to me. But that didn't make growing up any easier; if anything, all the passion flying around made it tougher. And being stoned on our asses most of the time didn't make things any simpler.

But on those perfect nights when we made love—yes!—until the dawn…

"I want to go to New York," I told him on one of those nights. "I want you to come with me."

After an unexpectedly long pause, he said, hand still on my dick, "I'm not sure."

Not sure? But didn't we love each other more than anything in the world? Well, sure we did. So I let that drop, didn't bring it up for the next couple of months. Winter finally thawed into spring, and we loved each other so much that even our straight friends suspected something was up, and then they knew for sure, and they, almost all of them, approved. Approved, maybe, in that "Man, go do your own thing" way, but that was fine all around.

As my graduation approached, his notion of moving to California, hanging out at the Fillmore, dancing to the Airplane and the Dead and Big Brother, seemed less and less attractive. I was raised to be an overachiever. It was hard to shake that. I wanted to be somebody. I wanted him to be part of that. My love.

So I suggested I go to New York, just to scout things out. If it didn't look promising, we'd try California.

But things in New York *did* look promising. Back then, the Manhattan underground was damn near as accessible as the subway, and it didn't take me too long to meet some of the cream of the avant-garde, up to and including the folks at Warhol's Factory. And if the underground's drug of choice was more often speed than acid, well, I could just steer clear. And anyway, I was hanging out with Billy Name and Taylor Mead.

The phone call when I told Charlie I wouldn't be coming back to Ohio didn't go well. Not well at all.

"I thought you loved me," he said.

"I do love you. More than anything. Come to New York and give it a chance. I already found a place for us. Really interesting apartment on Avenue B." I didn't mention its flourishing cockroach population.

"Without asking me?"

"Charlie, you have to learn to compromise."

He hung up.

I tried again, of course. Every time, the call went nowhere. I missed him a lot, needed him so much...but not so much I didn't seek the solace of other men at the baths. Eventually— well, actually pretty fast—the calls trailed off, and the last time I phoned, Charlie's number had been disconnected. I wrote a few letters, and though Charlie must have gotten them, since they never came back, I didn't receive a single reply. Anyhow, by that time, I'd already met Louis, a nurse who drank instead of using drugs, and who had a perfect body, much better than mine. Or Charlie's.

Time passed.

A lot of time.

It wasn't that I forgot about Charlie. You never forget your first love. A cliché, maybe, but true nonetheless. But there were others. A lot of others. And I loved some of them, as well. Louis, of course, but we didn't last all that long. And...well, others. Still, I thought of Charlie occasionally, wondering what had happened to him, what might have been.

And then, one beautiful spring day, a letter came for me. From Charlie.

I know I'm probably the last person you expected to hear

from after all these years, it read. *But you're kind of famous now, so it was no great problem finding out how to get in touch. And I'll be going to L.A. in a few weeks—ironic, I guess, that I ended up in New York, while you gravitated to the West Coast. I'd love to see you, catch up. No telling what might happen, but then, there are never any guarantees, are there? Anyhow, let me know. Love, Charlie.*

His using the L-word—twice—was both a little reassuring and a little worrying. And it set my heart, unbelievably, to racing.

The day he was due to arrive, I was all, embarrassingly, aflutter, like a teenage girl with a crush. I straightened up the apartment, shaved twice. Half-unconsciously, I put on an old Jefferson Airplane album.

At last the doorbell rang. Eighteen years later.

It was, unmistakably, Charlie. A bit heavier, with much shorter hair. But handsome, more handsome than I'd remembered. How could I have given him up? What a pointless question.

"Hey," he said, "how you doing?" He was looking straight at my wheelchair.

"I thought you knew," I said.

"I had no idea."

"I have no one to blame but myself. After the accident, I stopped drinking, been clean and sober ever since. But sometimes we learn too late."

"I guess." The words hung in the air.

"I don't work so well below the waist," I finally said, "but my mouth's still fine. If that's not too much information."

Charlie was silent.

"So how've you been?"

"Are you glad to see me?"

"Glad" didn't quite cover it. "Charlie..." I began. And then he leaned over and kissed me.

When the kiss ended, I could see there were tears in his eyes. Maybe in mine, too. Probably.

"Time's a bitch," I said.

"A bitch, yeah." He leaned back over and kissed me again. This time, the kiss lasted longer, went deeper.

Then Charlie knelt down by my chair and looked in my eyes. I'd forgotten about that shade of blue.

"You don't have to be afraid," he said.

"I'm not afraid." But I was.

Charlie began to stroke my useless legs. "Did you love me?" he asked.

"Yes, a lot. A whole lot."

His hands began to reach farther up, toward my crotch.

"Doesn't function so good anymore."

"Don't worry. It wasn't just about the sex, anyway. At least not for me."

"Me either. Or the drugs?"

"Or the drugs. Or the rock and roll, for that matter." Charlie smiled, that same dazzling smile. "And you're still one gorgeous stud."

"In this?"

Charlie leaned back and pointed to his crotch. "Swollen up, see?"

"I remember that you had a gorgeous cock. With a great foreskin. Am I wrong?"

"Have a look?"

"Please."

It was, in fact, beautiful, and not just because it belonged to the first man I fell for.

Okay, it seemed too soon, too easy, as though the years hadn't passed, as though what I'd done hadn't mattered. But Charlie was in my mouth, and I wasn't about to refuse his wet, salty gift.

Afterward, as I licked my lips, I had second thoughts. "This is stupid, really stupid," I said.

"Is it? No." Those blue eyes. "I don't think so."

"You're not going to leave me again?"

"You're the one who left me. Remember?"

I did. "And the chair?"

"I'm no prize package, either." And that smile. "You'll find out."

"I hope so," I said.

"You will."

I saw you. I saw you, coming back to me.

"I love you so fucking much," I said, "and I guess I always have."

Charlie smiled. Smiled.

WHAT WE LEAVE BEHIND

Shanna Germain

There is a dying dog the size of a small horse in my kitchen. She is nearly as tall as the kitchen table. Nearly as wide. With a hell of a lot more long white hair.

"I'm sorry," I say to the man who brought her here. "There's been a mistake."

The man who brought her is on his knees on my kitchen floor, rubbing the dog's brown- and gray-tipped ears. He has bits of gray in the dark hair above his own ears.

"It's okay, Annie," he says to the dog, who lets her tongue fall from her mouth and tilts her head sideways to listen. "This is gonna' be *sooo* good for you. Okay, girl, it's all good."

He doesn't seem to care that he's talking baby talk to this polar bear–like creature in front of me. He doesn't seem to hear me saying that the polar bear cannot stay in my kitchen.

When the man stands, his knees pop on the way up. "Ack, getting old." He shakes his legs out and laughs. "Too much bending down to dogs is more like it."

Even standing, he can't seem to keep his fingers out of Annie's fur. They nuzzle the pads of her ears while he pulls a clipboard from his shoulder bag.

I want to touch Annie, too. She's almost all white, except for those ears. From here, her fur looks like soft fuzz all over. But I don't touch her. I can't. It's not that she's dying. That, I'm used to. It's that she looks so damn healthy.

By the time Bella came to us, she was already missing her back leg from the knee down and was getting oral pain meds twice a day. Her owners had tried to save her by cutting off the tumored foot. But when the cancer spread, they decided it was too much and turned her over to the shelter. That's when she came to Thom and me.

It had been Thom's idea to take in a dying animal. A few years back, our local shelter had joined with a group of vets to start a hospice program for animals—some strays, some abandoned—who were dying, but still had quality time left in their lives. The goal was to get the animals into a good final home, a place where they could die with love and compassion. "We can still do something good," Thom had said when he'd heard of it. "Think of it, these animals, having to die alone."

He was thinking of himself too, of me after he was gone. That was after he got sick, but before we realized what it was. We'd thought it was AIDS, of course. As a gay man, you spend your whole adult life running from the thing you fear most, so fast that you don't see the other things on the way by. Until you get sideswiped by them. Car accidents. A guy in the alley with a knife. With Thom, it was lymphoma.

I'd said yes to the first dog—Bella, a lab-something-or-other—because I loved Thom, and I wanted to give him whatever I could, even at the end. Especially at the end. It made his skin ache to feel anything on it, but even so, it was Bella he let in the bed at night, Bella he reached for when the pain was bad. It was helping Bella toward her death that gave us something to focus on, that helped us move toward Thom's death in a way that felt, if not normal, no, never normal, at least like we were working with some kind of plan.

I didn't know that somewhere between those last days at home and his final trip to the ER he'd signed us—no, signed me—up for another dog.

I try again with the man in my kitchen.

"Really, I can't take her," I say.

He has finally let go of Annie's ears and is signing a clipboard with a big flourish. He holds the clipboard out to me.

"Of course you can," he says.

There is something in his dark eyes, a glimmer around the edges that shows he doesn't have any doubts. I signed on for this dog. She is here in my kitchen with two months to live. Of course I can take her.

I push the clipboard back at him. The ID tag clipped to his shirt pocket says, I'M A PAWSPICE VOLUNTEER! Beneath that it says, SETH.

"Listen, Seth," I say. "I can't take her. My partner signed us up and…" It is too complicated, too much to say. The words pile into my throat like bones and stick there.

Seth stays silent for a moment. Annie whines for the first time and pushes the side of her face carefully into his palm.

I feel like I have to say something, so I say, "I can't do it alone."

Seth holds the clipboard as though it's a Frisbee he'd like to wing at my head. I can understand the impulse. He probably sees this all the time—people who sign on for this venture and then decide they can't see it through.

But he doesn't wing the clipboard. He just says, "You

wouldn't be alone. You'd have Annie."

At the sound of her name, Annie pushes her cheek harder against Seth's hand. When she doesn't get a response, she turns her head my way. The kitchen is small, and she's so big that she nearly touches my thigh with her nose. Her eyes are so dark in all that white fur. I think what it would be like to have footsteps in the house again, noise at the door when I get back from errands. Somebody who needs me again.

I need time, so I ask, "What…what is she?"

Seth doesn't seem to notice my change in subject. Or perhaps he's content to ride it through.

"Great Pyrenees," he says. "Full-bred and papered." He doesn't say it with anger. He doesn't shake his head like I would have, to think of someone dropping off an animal, any creature, papered or not, just because it was terminal.

"Pyrenees?" I've never even heard of it.

Seth smiles for the first time. It's a half smile, shy enough to bring out dimples on both cheeks. "It's Norwegian for small horse," he says.

Annie wags her tail as though she gets the joke, and then drops herself to the kitchen floor at my feet. Her body makes a thud that's so loud I wonder if she's hurt herself, but she just puts her head down on her paws.

I stare at her. She looks so healthy. Thom and Bella both showed their illnesses. They were twins in the way their bodies responded. Losing weight no matter how much I fed them, until their knees were bigger than their thighs, until I could count every vertebra and rib with my fingers. Thom's fine blond hairs shedding on blankets next to Bella's dark curls. Neither of them said anything, not by mouth, but at the end, their bodies knew no language but pain.

This is what I think: *I can't do this again.*

This is what Seth seems to think: *He's going to do it.*

He is unpacking her things from his bag onto my kitchen table. The bag says, PAWSITIVELY PAWSPICE, in green letters with a big paw print on it. Like some kind of bizarre Mary Poppins, he pulls out two leashes, cans of dog food, an unopened package of very large bones, and a bottle of meds that rattles like maracas and makes Annie open her eyes warily.

"She doesn't need the meds very often," he says. "I don't think she likes the way they make her feel."

I nod. Thom complained of that all the time. The pain, he said, was easier than the disconnect. But then the pain would come on, hard, and he would let me open the IV, watch the liquid drip-drip him into semiconsciousness.

"She looks so healthy," I say. I don't even realize I'm going to say it.

"Nasal cancer," he says. "It's all on the inside."

"Nasal?" I'm not sure I know what that even means. I mean, I know what it means, but, "How does nose cancer land a dog on the hospice list?"

"It spreads," he says.

Seth keeps his eyes on Annie, who is, for the first time, starting to sound like a dog who might have something wrong with her. Her breath whines in, just a bit, only if you're listening in a quiet kitchen.

Seth reaches into his canvas bag and pulls out a tennis ball punched full of holes. Then he goes down on his knees next to Annie. I'm getting used to seeing the top of him like this. Even though it's not my own instinct, I like a man who will get down on his knees. Thom was a gardener, always in the dirt. Even near the end.

I realize that Seth is talking to Annie and to me at the same time.

"C'mon, girl, open up," he says. Then, to me, "Now, you'll want to catch her just before she falls asleep, and get the ball in her mouth. The holes help with the stridor, so she can breathe. She's used to it, so if you just ask her to open, she will. A bone works too, if you're out of tennis balls. Anything big enough to keep her mouth open while she sleeps."

Annie takes the ball in her mouth and drops her head back down on her paws. Her breathing is noticeably quieter.

Seth is still on his knees. I try not to look at his hands across her back. He has good wrists, muscled enough to chop vegetables and lift weights, soft enough to hold books and wineglasses by the stem.

Seth is still talking about Annie. "You could give her one of the pain pills, too, if she's having an especially hard time, but the tennis ball usually does the trick."

I realize I'm not listening. What I'm doing is eying Seth's back, the curve of his shoulders and hips. This realization makes me want to fuck and cry. While Thom was dying I looked at every-thing—everything—that walked by. I didn't touch; that was our rule. But, Jesus, I don't know if I'd ever been so horny in my life. We fucked some, then, almost to the end. Thom joked we were like pregnant women or little old ladies. He was afraid I wasn't attracted to him anymore; I was afraid to hurt him.

Near the end, sex took on this ritual: I would lie next to Thom, barely touching, and we would kiss. Just our lips and tongues. His lips still silver-soft from the lip balm he was addicted to. And then I would suck. As much as he was ashamed of his body at the end, he was always proud of his cock. I'm so grateful for that, that he had something to be proud of, always.

And I loved to suck him. The only part of his body that didn't lose its weight, that stayed full and heavy and alive in my mouth. I'd run my tongue up the ridges and veins, play over and over the soft curve of his head until his sighs changed from a long, slow release to a near-pant. Until he lifted his hips off the bed and put his fingers in my hair and said my name, over and over. And then, sometimes, he could fall asleep without the pain meds. Sleeping then, he looked like my Thom again. If I squinted, I could pretend I didn't see the IV poles, the hospital bed, the pill bottles, and tissues scattered around the living room. I could pretend he was just napping in the middle of the day.

And then the truth would come back and I'd go down to the laundry room and put already dry clothes in the dryer. Beneath the loud *clunk-clunk* of jeans and T-shirts, I'd masturbate, hard and fast, without lube, chafing my skin into some kind of pain. Sometimes I came. Sometimes I just cried.

But after Thom died, nothing. It was like my libido got dressed up in its best clothes, and lay down to be buried somewhere between Thom and Bella. For it to come back now, suddenly and with such force that my cock tightens in my jeans—it wrecks me.

I back away from Seth, trying to shift my legs to hide everything that's happening inside me. Seth raises his eyes to the triangle of my jeans. I turn away and grab the first thing my hand finds. One of Annie's tennis balls. When I squeeze it, the air shoots out the holes into my palm. I pick up the cans of food, put them into the cupboard, so I don't have to turn around.

"Well, I guess that's settled, then," Seth says to my back.

I'm not sure anything is settled, least of all me.

But I find myself stacking another can of food in the cupboard, saying, "I guess it is."

Even as Seth gathers his things, I keep my back turned. It isn't until he says, "I'll see you both in a week then," that everything subsides and I can turn and meet his dark eyes.

This, finally, is when I realize that somewhere between "I can't," and "You can," I've lost the battle. Annie is staying, and

this man is going to be back in my house in a week's time. And
I have no idea how to feel about either.

For the next six days, Annie and I try to get acquainted with
each other. She's learning to navigate the small house with her
big body, and I'm learning to get used to the sound of movement
in the rooms.

Every day, she chews her tennis ball at the back of my home
office while I build websites and answer emails. Every night, I
make up the bundle of blankets for her to sleep on in the living
room and every night, she stands at the foot of my bed watching
as I read or do crosswords or try not to think about Thom.
She doesn't whine or even beg. If she did, I think I could turn
her away, make it clear that the bedroom is not her space. But
she just watches me, tongue hanging, until I sigh and pat the
covers.

"C'mon then," I say. And she does. Crawls on her elbows
and knees across the covers like she's trying to make herself
smaller. Which is nearly impossible for a dog her size. Even the
bed lilts sideways at her weight. I give her one of the holey tennis
balls and she chomps on it for a while and then puts her head on
Thom's pillow to sleep.

So far, we haven't needed the drugs, and I think that makes
us both happy. It's a slippery slope, and slipperier at the end.
And although Annie's chart says five weeks, I know that could
mean anything. Bella lasted longer than she was supposed to.
Thom didn't.

Every morning, before our walk, I read the quality of life
checkpoints off to Annie. It's a lot of *h*'s and a few *m*'s. Hurt,
hunger, hydration, hygiene, happiness, mobility, more. It's
supposed to gauge how she's doing, what her quality of life is
like, if she's having more good days than bad.

I don't know if we got one of these for Bella. I'm sure we did, but I don't remember it. I wish I'd paid more attention. I wish I'd had a chart like this for Thom, although he probably would have thrown it across the room. He'd voted for calling the vet to put Bella to sleep as soon as she started showing real signs of pain, when she started having more bad days than good. But for himself, he wanted to hang in until the end, no matter the cost.

On our seventh day, the day that Seth is scheduled to come by for his check-in visit, Annie seems her usual tail-whipping self. Between breakfast and her walk, she manages to knock over the vase of yellow calla lilies that I bought…well, I won't let myself think why I bought them. The vase doesn't break, but the callas aren't salvageable.

Sometimes I swear she knocks shit over just to say that she's alive. Today, I wonder if she's not doing it to spite me for running the vacuum last night. Or maybe she's as nervous as I am about Seth coming. The way my body's jumping, if I had a tail, I'd be knocking crap off every surface, too.

I tell myself that I'm just nervous because I've gotten used to having Annie in the house, and he could decide it's not working out. But the truth is I'm excited, too.

"Okay, Missy," I say as I give both of us a once-over in the bedroom mirror—the tip of her tail is soggy from its run-in with the vase and I've got a squeaky toy tucked in my shirt pocket, but otherwise we look pretty good. "We need to make a good impression today," I tell Annie, who wags her tail at me.

And then Seth's knocking, calling. Annie and I nearly trip each other up trying to get to the door. Halfway across the kitchen, I calm myself and let Annie run ahead. Even so, when I swing the door open, we're both panting like fools.

Seth's standing there with a bone the size of Texas in one hand and what looks like a hand-picked bunch of black-eyed

Susans in the other. Annie looks back at me like she's smiling. I take a big gulp of air.

"Hey," I say.

"Hi," he says. I'm not sure if I noticed his smile last time, but I do now: straight white teeth, a full bottom lip that I want to suck.

We stand there while Annie's tail goes back and forth between the two of us. Seth holds out the bone.

"For you," he says to me.

We both look down at the huge thing in his hand.

Seth realizes what he's done. "Oh, ah…" he says. The tips of his ears darken with color. I'm not sure I've ever seen anything so sexy. He tries to switch hands, to offer the flowers instead, but I take hold of his wrist. I don't mean to. If I'd thought first, if a vision of Thom had entered my head, I would not have done it. But my body moved first, took his wrist, and now I'm holding the hand that's holding the bone.

"Come in," I say. His blushing, the way he fumbles through my doorway, are things Thom would never have done. I'm so grateful for the difference, for not having to compare him to Thom, that I pull him into the kitchen and press him back against the fridge. I find his mouth, that bottom lip, and I suck it into my mouth. He tastes of peppermint and basil.

Seth says something, but I can't tell what it is. It must be good, because his arms go around my back and he pulls me against him. The knotty end of the dog bone digs into my shoulder, but I don't care because our mouths are pressed together, our chests and cocks pushing into each other. He's big and the feeling of him through his jeans makes me grow large too.

I put my hands in his hair, feeling the soft black curls, the coarse gray strands. Jesus, I want to unbutton this man right here, I want to bend him over the kitchen counter and take him.

I try to tell him these things with my hips, the curve of my cock against his. He answers with his tongue, scraping the edge of my teeth, licking the inside of my cheek.

The fridge squeaks as Seth and I press into each other, harder and harder. The sound makes Annie bark, once, sharp.

All at once, we're a tangle of flowers and dog bone and tongues and panting. I step back, away from Seth's dark eyes. A flower petal brushes my ear as I break from his arms.

"I'm sorry," I say. "I don't know…"

He smiles, and for the second time today, I am aroused by straight, white teeth. He seems to have recouped his lost confidence. His face is still flushed, but I don't think it's embarrassment this time. My own cheeks feel overly warm.

Seth goes down on his knees to give Annie the bone. She pushes the healthy side of her face against his palm before she takes it between her teeth. Still on his knees, he holds out the slightly crushed bouquet of flowers. "Would you have a vase for these?" he asks.

We do what's civilized. I refill the calla vase with water and try to rearrange the flowers in a way that makes them look less like they were in the middle of a lust crush. And then I offer him lunch and he accepts.

I slice up cheese and salami. Pull yesterday's tomato and mozzarella salad from the fridge. He takes the knife I offer and slices a loaf of bread at perfect diagonals.

"Beer?" I ask.

He seems relieved.

"I'd love one," he says.

We eat while Annie gnaws her bone in the corner of the kitchen. We don't say much. It's the lunch of two men who were too nervous to eat all day. The lunch of two men who know that dessert is going to be the best—and longest—part of the meal. I watch his hands while he dips slices of bread into olive oil. I want to suck the oil from his fingers. Better yet, suck it from his tongue. But I hold myself steady. I eat. I mention how well Annie's doing. How healthy and happy she seems.

At the end, we clear the table as though we've been doing this for years. There is no sidestepping. Seth doesn't ask where the dishes go, or how to stack things. He just does. And then there is no more to do. Annie is asleep with the bone holding her jaws apart. Her breathing is nearly silent.

Seth straightens a towel that's hanging on the fridge. "What now?" he asks, without looking at me.

I touch his back, at the curve-in place just above his ass.

His voice low, still looking at the towel, Seth says, "I want you to fuck me."

It makes my cock pulse. Oh, Jesus. I bury my face in his neck. Even here, he smells of herbs.

"I want that, too," I say against his skin. I take his hand and pull him away from the towel rack. I mean to go to the living room, something less personal, but that's where Thom is, the memories of his last months and days, and I lead Seth into the bedroom instead. I think it surprises us both, this wide, carefully made bed waiting in the middle of the room.

Seth stops in front of it. I realize that if I stop now, I'll back out. I'll send Seth on his way, and Annie and I will live out the rest of her days in the safe, lonely rooms of this house.

Instead, I push my hands against Seth's chest. Somehow, in pushing him away, I pull him closer. My fingers open the buttons one by one. I'm shaking, and I have to hold on to each button tightly. Seth kisses my neck while I work. His hands slide down the back of me, from my shoulders to my waist. I hear my belt buckle open, feel the warmth as he slides it from my jeans.

Everything's too slow for me.

"Please undress. I want to see you," I say.

Seth lets go of my jeans. He undresses quickly, dropping his clothes in piles. His body is lean but muscled. His cock swings up, long and thin, the smooth head a beautiful pinky-purple. His body is so alive, so much muscle and blood pumping, that I'm afraid to touch him.

It doesn't matter. He comes to me, undresses me as fast as he did himself. Even so, I marvel at his hands everywhere: buttons, sleeves, sliding my underwear down my thighs so my cock springs up.

"Oh," he says. And he never comes up from taking my underwear off. He stays on his knees, and I can see the lean muscle of his back, and just below that, the perfect curves of his ass. He licks his lips and presses them to the head of my cock.

It's been so long since I've felt anything other than my own hand that just the press of his lips there makes me want to grab the back of his head and fuck his mouth. I try to keep still. When he opens his lips, lets me slide inside him, against the press of tongue and teeth, it's almost too much. I grit my teeth to stem the rising pleasure. His tongue finds the sweet spot just beneath my head, laps at it.

"Ah, Jesus," I say. Through my gritted teeth, it comes out as something less awed, more primal. I pull Seth up from his knees. His lips are cherry red and wet. He licks a drop of precum from his big bottom lip.

"What are you doing to me?" I ask, even as I'm laying him down on his back on the bed. He doesn't answer. He doesn't have to. The way his cock jumps as I position myself over him, the way he puts his legs up to give me access, says it all.

I lick my finger and use it to find the swirl of his asshole. I press against it, and Seth opens for me, already pushing down on my finger.

"More," he pants. I enter with a second finger, let his body settle over it. He wraps his fingers tight around the base of his cock. The color darkens even more. My cock is jumping every time Seth's ass tightens around my fingers. It wants in. I want in.

"Seth, I want..."

"Yes," he sighs. "Yes."

I fumble in the nightstand drawer for lube and condoms, hoping there's something left over. Hoping I won't break down when my hand hits a cellophane wrapper.

Thankfully, Seth puts his other hand around my cock. He's wet his palm and his fingers slide over my skin, slick enough to take my mind off everything that came before this moment. I find a half-empty bottle of lube and one lonely condom in the bottom of the drawer.

Seth wraps his fingers around the base of my cock while I roll on the condom. He tightens his grip, a human cock ring that makes me pump my hips against his hand as I spread lube over the surface.

"It's cold," I say.

Seth's already raising his hips to me, the perfect circle of his asshole waiting.

"Don't care," he says.

I push my way inside him. Just the head at first. How much I've missed this entering is something that I feel in my whole body. This is how I try to be: Slow. Careful. But Seth is sucking me in with his low moans, with his fingers tight on my ass.

The slide inside is: *Oh, fuck.* And then I'm buried in him, his ass contracting and releasing around me. I stop.

"I don't know how long I'm going to last," I say. "I can't promise—"

Seth pulls my face down to his, offers me that big bottom lip to suck on. It shushes me.

"Just fuck me," he says against my mouth.

I do, oh, god, I do. Rising and falling inside him. Seth pushes his hips upward to meet my thrusts. We are greedy together, wanting it all.

And then I close my eyes, just for a second, and see Thom's face. For some reason, it's okay, though; he looks happy. Or at least he doesn't look unhappy.

When I open my eyes, Seth is pumping his cock at the same rhythm as I'm fucking him. His head is thrown back, and he moans low. It's visceral: the sound, the feeling of his hot skin around me. I come.

Coming is like this: Everything emptying. Everything filling. The long, slow release of something I've been holding on to for too long. It is liquid leaving and me becoming liquid and the way Seth says "Aw, god," and Annie's low whine from the other room.

When I wake up, I've got a big white paw in my face, and I realize that while we were sleeping, Annie must have crawled in bed.

Seth's already awake. His fingers are back in the fur at Annie's ear.

"I need to tell you something," he says.

My soul says: *Oh, shit.* My mind says: *Wait and listen.*

"I got assigned to you on purpose," he says.

"What?"

Seth drops his eyes, pretends to pick something out of Annie's fur. And then his words come out in a tumble.

"Thom came into the shelter in person when he signed up. He was so sweet, told us the whole story. He wanted you to have something after. It was supposed to be sooner, that's what he wanted, but there wasn't a good match. I asked to be assigned to you."

I shift Annie's paw off my shoulder, lean up a little. "Is that kind of creepy?" I ask.

The tips of Seth's ears are growing a dark red. I can't help it. I think of his cock.

"Maybe," he says. "But Thom was so nice, and I thought, 'A man who's in love with this man must be amazing, too.' I just wanted to see if it was true."

"And?"

He swallows audibly. The sure man who was in my bed minutes ago has disappeared.

"And...you were not only nice, but you were so sexy. I got sucked in."

His lip is pouting out so far I'm tempted to bite it.

Instead, I ask, "Would you like to get sucked in again?"

The tips of his ears still showing red, he nods.

I run my finger along the edges of his lips.

"Let me feed the small horse, then," I say. "And when I come back, I'll see what I can do."

It's been three months and two days, and Seth has moved in. He's brought his life with him: paperwork and photos from Pawspice, a shed full of gardening tools, his ability to grow herbs and tomatoes like he's made of fertilizer.

Annie's days are switching from mostly good to mostly bad. Something has speeded up inside her, is pushing her quickly toward the end. Five times a day, we coax her to eat by cupping Alfredo sauce in our palms and letting her lick it out.

This morning, while Seth cooks breakfast, I mix up the solution to wash Annie's coat—mostly water, a little lemon juice, and hydrogen peroxide. She lies on the rug in the kitchen, the ball between her teeth. She has it almost all the time now, and still she needs the meds.

I wring out the sponge—my skin is permeated with the scent of lemons—and I run it carefully over Annie's face. She closes her eyes when I get near her nose, and I talk low to her, tell her I'm sorry if I hurt her.

Seth chop-chops the onions on the board. The room smells of acid and tears.

"I think it's almost time," I say. I'm talking to Annie and to Seth. Somehow, they both nod.

Not today, not tomorrow, but soon, we will lose Annie and all she has brought to us. Well, not everything she has brought to us. We'll still have: Memories. Tennis balls filled with holes in every room in the house. A bed that sags on one side. Each other.

THE CALAMUS EMOTION: LOVE AMONG THE RUINS

Jack Fritscher

San Francisco, April 25, 1906

Dear Benny,

It's yer old (ha ha) pal Jimmy writin you from General Delivery in Frisco where you might of heard back in Saint Louie we had a little earthquake on my birthday Wednesday last, April 18. What a way to turn nineteen (ha ha). No cake for me like two years ago at our fine spree at the Saint Louie World's Fair before I lit out for Frisco on the train from Union Station. I ain't forgot that cake or the icin on it. How we had our cake & ate it too. Sorry I ain't writ you much but I bin thinkin about you, &, pal o mine, I wish you were here, but I'm glad you ain't been through what I been through. What I seen in the last seven days could break a man's heart. This whole city it ain't gone, but sorely wounded. Ma Sloat's boardin house where I live is all charcoal ashes down South of the Slot, along with all the South of Market buildins around it. So forget that address.

It were all us workin men livin in cheap rooms down there, & pore families, cuz nice San Franciscans never cross South of the Slot in Market Street. Remember I toll you last letter how the iron cable-car slot worked, runnin down the center of Market Street, pullin the streetcars from the Ferry Buildin west toward Twin Peaks like a hummin metal line fencin off us & the rich folk we work for. It were terrible after the shakin woke us all up at 5:12 in the A.M., yellin in our longjohns, steppin out as I did from my third-floor window that crumpled down like a house of cards to the curb, crushin fellas livin under me, all us who could dashin out into the cold streets, everyone screamin. The *Chronicle* says 60,000 of us souls live down South of Market, & we was all runnin for it, tryin to get away from the fire that started in a Chinee laundry near Ma Sloat's at Third & Brannan. It just spread & spread through all the broken wood & gas mains shootin flames into the air. At 8:14 A.M. come another quake rollin through, knockin more buildins down like tinder, & puttin folks chokin on all the smoke in a worse panic.

I don't want to make you sick, dear Benny, but there was women and children, whole families killed, and lots of men, more than you can guess. Lots of fellas, some of em I knew, trapped in the collapse of all the bachelor workmen's boardin houses. They saw the path of the fire and they was beggin, shoutin, you could hear, in all kinds of languages, at first for somebody to pull em out, till those that didn't have guns to kill themselves, becuz they was about to be burned to death, was beggin somebody, anybody to shoot em, & they was shot. Some of em as a mercy was shot by each other, you could see em, some dyin naked as they was born, & even if you turned away, you could hear the shots that stopped the shouts. I didn't need the priest from Saint Pat's, which toppled down, kneelin in the holy bricks prayin in the middle of Mission Street, to tell me it was a vision of hell, & I was glad he got up like a man & started pullin trapped souls out from the rubble. Nothin none of us could do to keep somethin like 3000 souls alive in our disaster. Somethin like 500 looters, & still countin, was shot on site includin 2 fellas I knew who was just tryin to get their trousers & shoes & pocket watches & tintypes out of the wreckage. Gunfire & flames & smoke & explosions & the ground quiverin every few minutes like the earth was a bag of gravel. I left Ma Sloat's hightailin it with nothin.

Don't know where I'm gonna live. Am now sleepin rough, in a view with no room, you might say, as I'm campin on leaves of grass in a make-shift lean-to against one a the thousands of tents in Golden Gate Park which you may recall I once toll you you'd like since I could see us walkin there, hand in hand through Paradise.

You mayhaps have already read in the Saint Louie *Post-Dispatch* how when our Opera House fell down around his eyetalian ears, the Great Caruso sat on the ground in Union Square & cried, with less courage than Pagliacci's "Vesti la Giubba," that he was never comin back to Frisco. The tent my lean-to's presently up against in the Park sports a "hoochie-koochie" sign from downtown readin "Maiden Lane" (ha ha), & the friendly "tootsie-wootsies" inside it, who I do-for (cuz among their services to other fellas) they cook for me, have been laughin at Caruso as not bein all that great! They hear tell that the grand soprano Luisa Tetrazzini herself, who don't scare easy like her warblin tenor chum Caruso, is sometime soon headin back into Frisco to sing free at Lotta Crabtree's fountain which is about the only thing still standin downtown at Market & Geary. The ladies, who know a town pump when they see one, been cookin what they been jokin is "Chicken Tetrazzini" in her honor. I toll em it should be "Chicken Caruso," & they all laughed, & give me pie. So life ain't all bad, or bad at all, & it's startin over, life is, which is the secret of Frisco.

I was wondrin if you wanted to come out here to the ruins (ha ha, but I mean it) cuz you said you were needin work & there's lots of it here now, even more than before, for thousands of us strong young fellas.

Which vision reminds me I been takin my salt-water sea-bathing, 7 A.M to 6 P.M., once-a-week out near the ocean, at cold North Pacific temperatures & up to eighty degrees, for twenty-five cents at the Sutro Baths that's all glass and iron as fine as any building at the Saint Louie Exposition. Reason enough for you to travel west, there's bathing music performed by the Sutro Baths Band, & I bet we could work for room & board for that ol blonde Ma Sloat nobody calls "Ma Slut" to her face. She's rebuildin over on Folsom Street upstairs over where her brother Hallam has a piece of property for a new saloon cuz he believes in the future of Frisco even South of the Slot. She says he believes in the future of thirst, & he be namin the little street next his after their father the older Hallam who ain't unlike yer pa & mine when it comes to bellyin up to a bar to bend an elbow.

If you have work there in Saint Louie then maybe you could send yer old secret chum a couple bucks to help out, but, dear Benny, if I have to start over, & I do have prospects, I'd a damn sight rather start over with you by my side here in Frisco cuz you never know what's gonna happen next, but this monkey's uncle, yours so truly, can tell it's gonna happen here, & it could be good for us. Remember when you was seein me off at the train station, steamin away, you cracked wise that confirmed bachelors gotta know how to take care of ourselves.

I can't meet you in Saint Louie, Louie, where we fell down laughin tryin to dance the hoochie-coochie, but I can meet you at the Golden Gate. Don't be late! You might want to hear the

Great Tetrazzini as much as me (ha ha) except this boy ain't
no more singin soprano. That married bachelor Horace Greeley
was right when he said, Go West, young man, Go West! There's
gold in them thar hills! I found, down near the Embarcadero,
blowin around on Folsom Street, some French postcards like
you never seen. It's an ill wind that blows no good instructions.

I love this place, but not as much as you know who. There.
I finally said what you said when last we parted. Put that in yer
pipe, dear Benny, & smoke it. Two bucks would be fine. Yer
hand in mine, pal o mine, would be better. If I had a ceilin, I'd
be lyin awake at nights starin at it & thinkin of you, takin it all
in hand, your hand in mine, hand in glove with you.

Yer devoted pal,

Jimmy

ADULT

Natty Soltesz

S ess Roberts wiped a glob of bluish-white cum off of the wall and tried to recall the allure a porno-clerk job once held for him. There was more cum on the floor of the stall (or "buddy booth," as they called the enclosures) but he let that go. He had nine more to clean and he was tired.

He could hear obscene wet sloshing coming from dedicated regular Lloyd Donahue's stall as he zipped past. Lloyd had given up approaching Sess after the fourth or fifth week, for which Sess was thankful, but it was better to avoid contact if at all possible, especially since they were the only ones in the store. At least he wouldn't have to clean up Lloyd's load until tomorrow morning; all the better to let his germs dissipate a little.

It wasn't like he'd ever held illusions about the job—he'd known what he was getting into. For nearly a year before he applied for work he'd been adding his own DNA to the wealth of genetic material on the arcade walls, when it wasn't being guzzled down by the minivan-and-wedding-band set, that is.

He dumped the pail of scummy water in the back room sink and stepped outside for a smoke. The dark highway lay before him, stretching out in both directions. Maybe it was silly, but the highway was part of what drew him to the job. It was four A.M., that netherworld between night and morning. Every other minute or so a car would fly by in a red and white streak, leaving a lonely sound in its wake. Who were they? Where were they going? He was just a blip, a speck on a point on a map. But even in the smallest of places there were huge things happening, whole worlds nobody would ever know about.

He snubbed out his cigarette in a coffee can nailed to the shelter that hid the front entrance from the highway. He heard a motorcycle—a Harley—approaching. It slowed as it neared the building and turned into the parking lot.

Sess ducked inside, behind the counter. The bell rang as the biker walked inside, then turned toward him and smiled. That was unusual. Most patrons slithered behind the shelves and never made eye contact. The biker's grin was big and handsome. If Sess hadn't been so taken off guard he would've smiled back.

"Howdy," the biker said. He was in his forties. He was hot.

"Can I help you?"

"I hope so," he said in a gravelly voice, resting his golden brown arms on the counter. "Do you know how far it is to Cleveland?"

"Cleveland? Jesus—no. I think at least three hours, maybe four?"

"You ever been there?"

"No."

The biker stretched, raising his arms over his head. His leather jacket and black T-shirt rode up, exposing a thick, tan stomach.

"Oh, well," he said. He reached into his pocket. "Ten tokens please." Sess poured the tokens into his hand. "Long night for ya?"

"Long enough," Sess answered.

"Tired, huh?"

"A little."

"I'm gonna get some relief myself," the biker said. He winked, then vanished into the dark arcade.

Sess had known about the porno store since he was young; everyone in Groom did. It was on Route 428, right on the edge of town. The sign alone screamed sex; pitch-black letters on a lit-up yellow background that simply said ADULT. Mothers would try to shame ingoing patrons by honking their horns as they drove past, and concerned women had led campaigns over the years to shut it down. Still it stood, a monument to the elephant in everyone's rooms. The women knew what went on in there, or thought they did. The point was that they thought about it.

What Sess hadn't known about was the arcade. He'd found out about that through a website, cruisingforsex.com, staring in open-mouthed wonder at the computer screen to see that here, in the tiny nowhere town of Groom, Pennsylvania, there was not one but *two* places listed where people could go for anonymous gay sex.

He'd tried the other place first—Promised Land State Park, which was just up the highway from Wal-Mart. He spent some time hanging around in his mom's Cavalier and later on the playground swings, dragging his feet on the ground. One guy walked past him. He wore a windbreaker and had beady eyes, and as soon as Sess made eye contact he knew. The guy hung around the parking lot, but Sess didn't know what to do so he ignored him. He was relieved when the guy left.

Being underage, he'd had to work up some nerve to try the

porno store. He walked there the first time, fearful of someone spotting his mom's Cavalier. It was a good twenty-minute walk from his house, along a backcountry road that ended right at the highway, the porno store about fifteen yards from that. To stay out of view, he crept along the sharply sloping hillside behind the store, twisting his ankle and slashing his arms on thorny branches.

The lot behind the store, shielded from the highway and ringed by the woods, was a world unto itself. Yellow sodium lights had kicked on in the waning evening light, illuminating at least five cars, four with men sitting inside. Their eyes followed Sess as he nervously opened the back door.

The adult store, inside, was both thrillingly alien and disappointingly mundane, mainly white shelves lined with videos and DVDs. The boxes displayed colorful pictures of pink holes and engorged organs. The fluorescent lighting made it look like Rite-Aid, only with dildos.

The overweight guy behind the counter (the owner, he'd later find) looked at him as he entered. Sess braced himself for the worst. But the guy just smiled; an icky smile that let Sess know exactly what he was thinking.

Sess had never considered himself a good-looking kid. He was tall and gangly, with flat, black, boring hair and a jaw that sloped into his neck rather than jutting out. But it didn't take long to sense that here he was the belle of the ball. Had this been a cartoon the clerk would have had a thought bubble of a steaming, freshly cooked chicken hovering over his head. He didn't card Sess, didn't say anything but, "Have a good time," and handed him his tokens.

Sess thought about heading into the arcade to cruise the biker. Sex on the job was expected, even encouraged by the owner, who'd addressed it during his interview.

"Just do it in the center booth and keep the door open a little so you can see if anybody's trying to steal shit," he'd said. He took Sess on a tour of the place, principally to corner Sess in a booth and take out his cock. It was impressive and would've been intriguing had it not been attached to such a repugnant person.

"It's nice," Sess demurred, then pushed past the guy. He may have been naïve but he was not about to blow a big-titted greaseball for a porno-shop job.

Sess heard Lloyd shuffling around in the arcade and hoped the biker had sense enough to turn the old troll away. Truth was, he wasn't sure about the biker. He'd gathered a good deal of experience with cruising in the past year, but something about the biker threw him off. He seemed too confident, too self-contained. Sess wondered if he was straight.

He feared rejection. A few weeks after Sess had started coming to the arcade, he'd screwed up enough courage to approach a hot college guy around his age, a rarity in the place. The guy sat there, looked him up and down, and simply shook his head as though Sess was one of a choice of entrée selections that he didn't care for. The sympathetic look Lloyd gave him on his way back to his booth only made it worse.

So the biker went about his business in the dark and Sess kept behind the counter, watching the goings-on in the back lot via a black-and-white monitor mounted under the counter. The owner didn't care if people cruised out there, but he liked to keep an eye on things. Sess watched a car drive in, poke slowly through the mostly empty lot, and continue on its lonely way.

The porno store became a refuge for Sess during his last year of high school, a safe house for some beleaguered central part of him that most everyone—his asshole Catholic parents especially—wanted to ignore. The store was his burning secret, the sly smile on his face when he walked down the chaotic halls of Groom Senior High. The sexuality that had lain dormant and unacknowledged since junior high was now alive and kicking and powerfully real.

He didn't have any friends in high school, just acquaintances. He wore black and listened to Nine Inch Nails and cultivated a personality that was above and beyond humanity. He got harassed a lot, even early on. It was like they could sniff it out. By his junior year people were harassing him in class, coughing "fag" under their breath. They practically knew before he did.

The worst was Dan Frye, running back for the Groom Bobcats and Chief Asshole of the school. He'd hone in on Sess in the hallway, approaching him slowly, getting closer so that the minute their sides touched he could slam hard against Sess's shoulder, knocking him off balance and spinning him around. He'd put his lips to Sess's ear and in a throaty snarl he'd say the magic word.

Dan wasn't like the others. He didn't need a crowd or an audience; he wasn't making fun or provoking laughter. That was what made him so dangerous. For him it was personal. It was serious.

Which made it all the sweeter when Sess fucked Dan's dad just prior to graduation.

That day had started out with frustration. His parents were gone for the weekend, and the lilting promise of unquestioned hours away from home had been crushed hard by an unusually desolate Friday night in the arcade. For what felt like hours he fed tokens into the TV, nobody but Lloyd and the usual suspects cruising past his booth, hoping for a bite. Then a new guy passed his booth. For a split second he looked in, caught Sess's eye, and that was all it took.

Sess had noticed Dan Frye's dad before. It was sort of impossible not to. The guy was built like a battleship, exhibiting his body with impunity in tight polo shirts with buttons undone, the smooth hard mounds of his cleavage eclipsing his wife's, his beefy butt encased like sausage meat in his jeans, a healthy crotch packed tight up front. He was a stud, plain and simple, and had the same air of cocky assholery as his son.

Sess crept up to his stall. The sliding door of the older man's booth was open and he stuck his head inside. Tom Frye was sitting on the small bench across from the TV, watching straight porn. He looked at Sess (he didn't seem to recognize him) and grabbed his crotch as an invitation. Sess stepped inside and slid the door shut. He thought he heard Lloyd's dejected sigh.

Sess knelt on the floor. He unbuckled Tom's pants, revealing stylish black bikini briefs. The older man was completely hard. Sess took it out. Tom drew air in through his nose, his head back and his eyes closed. His cock wasn't all that large, but that wasn't the point. His pubes were trimmed to a neat crew cut; his balls were shaved. Sess wondered if Dan's cock was similar.

He slid it down his throat. Tom didn't make a sound. A pass, another pass, and already Tom's legs were tensing up, so Sess backed off. He tapped Tom under his arms, and Tom got the message and stood up. Despite the guarded, hostile air Tom gave off in public, he was pliant and accommodating inside the booth, in the moment. He let Sess turn him around and strip the briefs from the firm mounds of his butt. Sess caressed the ass like it was a crystal ball. This was an absolute coup.

Eating a guy out was something Sess had only fantasized about. He went for broke, burying his face in Mr. Frye's butt. Tom couldn't suppress an overwhelmed whimper. He leaned his head against the wall, supporting it with his arm, and keeping his eyes shut tight. Sess tongued Tom's crack good but the asshole never truly relaxed. It remained tight and tense, even when Sess wormed a finger inside.

He grabbed lube and a condom out of his jeans pocket, took his pants down, and got himself ready. Tom said nothing, just kept his ass backed up as Sess mounted him and worked the head of his dick inside, probably being rougher than he should have, but Tom didn't object.

The porn on the monitor lit up their sex in shifting phosphorescent patterns. Sess, a kid who wasn't even a blip on Tom's radar—but who loomed large on the son's—was now inside a shrine to masculinity, defiling him, using him like a whore. He barely noticed when Tom climaxed, the cum spilling out of his untouched dick and pooling on the bench. Sess came soon after, inside the condom, inside Dan Frye's dad. He might as well have been erecting a flag on the surface of the moon.

Graduation passed and his eighteenth birthday came and Sess applied that very day and got the job. The fact that his parents hated it made it that much sweeter. They threatened to kick him out of the house.

"Do it," he said, eating his Frosted Flakes, knowing they would never. He was their only child, the buffer for their anxieties in a loveless marriage, and without him they'd collide and fall apart.

His shift was from eleven P.M. to six A.M., during which time he sampled from a wholly exhaustible succession of cocks, mouths, and assholes. Only recently had it grown stale, all the secrecy and shame and cum for cum's sake. When they were done they zipped up and got out, went home to their wives and their beaten-down lives, their throats raw from sucking him off, their hands cramped from milking his precious elixir, for wasn't he the fountain of fucking youth? Couldn't his cum restore them to a life of promise and vitality, a time before children and mortgages and exercise equipment that collected dust in the basement rec room?

His cum was a truth serum for those living a lie.

He wiped it away every shift, wasted potential spackled to the stalls and drooling off the walls. How long did it take for sperm cells to die?

The biker spent half an hour in the arcade. When he emerged he looked almost hurt. He walked up to the counter.

"Nice booths you got there," he said.

"They're okay."

"I guess you've seen enough of this place."

"Pretty much, yeah."

The biker looked down at his boots. He raised his head. "I'm Ron," he said, holding out his hand. Sess shook it. It was tough and solid. It had integrity. Sess introduced himself.

"Cleveland, huh?" Sess said.

"Yep. Thought I'd make it there tonight but guess not. Maybe I oughta crash here—is there a motel nearby?"

"Yeah, there's a Best Western about ten miles west."

"Care to join me?" he said.

"I'm working," Sess said, laughing. Ron brightened. He'd cracked Sess's armor.

"When do you get off?"

"Six."

"Hmm...don't know if I can hold off that long."

"You didn't do anything in the booth?"

"I mean hold off without sleep. But no, I didn't do anything in the booth. I was hoping you'd stop by."

"We could still," Sess said, already walking around the counter. Ron stepped up to him. For a moment Ron let the sizzling space between their bodies be. Then he took the younger man in his arms and kissed him. Sess had never been kissed before. Sex, yes. Passion, no. They broke apart and Ron shot him a widescreen grin. *Funny*, Sess thought, *how you never notice the absence of things.*

They went into the arcade. Lloyd was still in the center stall so they took a back booth. He wouldn't be able to monitor the front, but he was past that. Ron reached down to feel his package and looked at him in surprise. He'd found Sess's secret weapon. They massaged each other through their jeans for a while, making out and staying so, so close.

Ron went down on him. He had technique, taking Sess's cock in slowly, savoring every inch, letting it fill his throat before sliding back up. He kept his eyes on it, massaging Sess's balls, then hungrily going down on it again, and Sess felt it in his toes. Ron breathed heavily through his nose as he worked Sess's dick, his tongue thickly slathering the underside.

He heard the bell ding on the door and realized Lloyd had left. Ron stood up and freed his cock. It was fat, stout, perched atop two hearty balls under a nest of dark hair. Sess took it in his hand and dropped to his knees. It was a suckable cock and Sess took full advantage of its party size. Ron was a leaker. Sess liked that. He licked it right off of Ron's cockhead, hot and fresh.

He felt Ron's body, tight and smooth with a smattering of hair across his chest. He tweaked Ron's nipples and the biker moaned. The moans cut through the silence of the store. Normally you didn't make any noise, but it was just them, just now.

Ron turned around and dropped his black jeans over his butt, which was smooth as an egg and nut brown in color.

"You're so tan," Sess said.

"I like to ride naked whenever possible," Ron said. He kicked off his jeans and widened his stance, revealing a buttcrack lined with fine hair that ringed around his pink asshole.

Sess ate him out. Ron's butt was clean but sweaty from a day spent on the road. He tentatively touched a finger to Ron's hot hole, trying to gauge his reaction. Ron reached back, took hold of his hand, and pressed Sess's finger inside of him. He was tight and hot.

"You wanna fuck me?" Ron said.

"Sure," he said. Ron smiled.

"You got a rubber?"

"Definitely." Pants still around his ankles he shuffled into the store, coming back with supplies. Ron laughed.

"I'll need to sit on it first," he said. Sess got on the bench and let Ron lower himself onto his cock. He was facing him as he did it and Sess watched his expression, the hot flash of pain as Sess's cock first pierced inside, then a gradual letting go until he was bouncing up and down on Sess, his hard cock bobbing in time.

"How do you want me?" he asked.

"Huh?"

"How do you wanna fuck me? From behind?"

"Okay."

So he fucked Ron doggy-style. Only then did he realize they were in the same booth in which he'd fucked Dan Frye's dad. The same thing—fucking—but it was completely different. Where Tom had been stiff and scared, Ron was loose and free, backing up to meet his thrusts, reaching back to grab Sess's ass and pull him in deeper.

Sess had yet to bottom with a real dick. And though he'd experimented with whatever phallic-shaped object was lying around the house, he thought that anal sex wasn't something a guy with a dick up his ass enjoyed—it was being dutiful, an act of martyrdom. For Tom Frye it had been a chore, a dirty deed. Ron got fucked right up into a higher plane of existence.

"I'm gonna cum," Ron said, and his hand clenched around Sess's asscheek. He found Sess's hole with his finger and pressed it tight. Sess cupped his palm in front of Ron's dick and caught his load. He brought it to his tongue and it tasted good. He lapped it up as he power-fucked the biker, swallowing it as Ron's finger pressed into his ass and he started losing it himself. His knees went weak as spurt after spurt of jizz filled the condom in Ron's ass.

Ron kissed him again when they broke apart.

Sess got some paper towels. "Thanks," Ron said, as Sess wiped the lube from his butt.

"Just doing my job." He got dressed and scanned the store. No damage, no foul.

"Let's talk," Ron said as he swaggered out of the arcade, still buckling his belt. "What are you doing these days?"

"What do you mean?"

"I'm headed west. On my bike. There's a place in California, just south of San Francisco. A little beach town, some friends of mine have a community out there." Sess looked at Ron. "There's room on the bike," he said, smiling. "I think you should come with me."

"Right now?"

"If you want. But I need some sleep. Tomorrow, then. Early."

"I have to work tomorrow."

"Not *really*," Ron said. "You don't *have* to do anything except eat and shit and live and die, right?"

"I live with my parents."

"I'll pick you up there."

"I only have a couple hundred bucks."

"That's enough," Ron said. Sess shuffled his feet. "Give me your address," Ron said. "I'll stop outside tomorrow. Nine A.M., so don't sleep late. I'll honk the horn and if you don't come out I'll keep going." Sess wrote his name and address on a receipt. "Sess. I thought you were saying Seth. My last name's Wood; friends call me Woody."

They shook hands. Ron put a hand on his shoulder and looked in his eyes.

"Don't think about it," he said. He leaned forward, gave him another kiss, and took off. The sound of his Harley faded as it cruised down the highway.

Sess looked at his empty store. He knew what he wanted to do in his heart, but that was such bullshit. People said, "Follow your heart," like it was an easy thing to do. There was a lot of space between your heart and your brain, a lot of bundled up nerves and connections that didn't always carry the message.

He thought about his dog at home, Cougar, so loving and loyal. The minute Sess walked in the door Cougar would wrap around his legs in ecstatic circles. He'd curl up next to him in bed as he slept, whether it was for a couple of hours or until late afternoon.

He thought about Cougar and he started to cry, right there in the store, because his bags were already packed. He was gone.

BRIEFLY, FOREVER

Lee Houck

In the summer of 1998, I was working in Vermont as an unpaid and mostly underfed puppeteer. Everyone was hanging out around the fire, rolling cigarettes, rolling joints; the moon stretched the shadows into long thin lines. I watched the oddly matched couples slink away from the light, their tangled silhouettes growing dimmer and dimmer. It suddenly occurred to me that the people who I would find myself hanging out with for the rest of my life would be people who voted for the Democratic candidate because he was the lesser evil. Some of them would write in Angela Davis. Some of them would not vote at all. They would dress in unfashionable clothing, drink whisky from plastic cups in their living rooms, and go contra dancing. They would drink expensive coffee carried across borders by Fulbright scholars and drive cheap cars.

It occurred to me, when I found myself alone, staring at the cooling embers, that I had made a mistake. At some point in my life, years earlier perhaps, I had decided what kind of people I would meet, what kind of theater I was going to create, and how much or how little I was going to get emotionally involved.

There at the fire, I asked myself: *What happens if you give in to it?*

If you laugh at all the jokes, slather your arms in papier mâché and printing ink, devour the over-toasted granola, skip laundry, skip the shower, skip the telephone calls, go to the too-late parties, go skinny-dipping, go to town and be stared at by the locals.

And what happened after all that, after diving in, was this:

He was one of about ten students who had come to Vermont from a theater school in Mexico City. They were dancers, singers, actors, and sometime musicians who spoke varying degrees of English, who I met in a line, one after another, repeating my name then theirs back to them, not remembering a single one. He was barely taller than me, with a thinner build. His English was terrible; I spoke no Spanish. We carried a dictionary with us, and learned a truncated way of flipping through the pages to get the nouns and crudely miming the actions. My flashlight broke, it was too dark to fix it, and we kissed for the first time. We fooled around in his tent under blankets, army issue, heavy and brown. We woke up, covered in wool fuzz that was indelibly stuck to our bodies where they had been moist with lube— hands, nipples, crotches. The next evening, after the first full day of performances (from about ten in the morning to eight at night) we actually fell asleep during sex. We'd had little to eat all day, carrying giant puppets across the fields all that afternoon, and after rolling around in the tent for about fifteen minutes at nearly one in the morning, we paused to breathe (or paused to hear what our bodies were feeling, like you can do during sex) and fell right asleep. Neither of us could remember who did so first.

Some other puppeteers, a Parisian woman and her Canadian boyfriend, drove us to Boston, where my charming Mexican's second cousin lived with his American wife, a nurse who cooked amazing dinners. We bought a plant for their apartment. We slept on the pullout bed in the living room, and he was afraid that she'd walk in on us sleeping, cuddling together on one side of the bed. We took a shower together in their bathroom and, though I'd seen him naked a dozen times, he asked me to look away when he undressed. We cooked elaborate dinners with our puppeteer friends, with spicy corn salad, leeks in crème fraiche, plum-glazed pork loin, and perfect French bread from the Jewish bakery.

We came to my New York apartment, shared my twin-sized bed, and that was when he prayed—on his knees, right there on the floor of my bedroom, both of us naked, my erection suddenly deflating—before giving me a blow job. He had to go back to Mexico on September third. He would take a bus to the Newark Airport.

We knew what it was. I wouldn't write him. I wouldn't call him. It was simply going to be over. He left at nearly four o'clock in the morning. I was still asleep.

I won't tell you his name, though I remember it completely—it's like a secret that I keep to myself, or a place I keep sentimental things hidden. I remember carrying cardboard and papier mâché puppets across the freshly mowed dairy fields littered with garlic peel and paint flecks. I remember lying in the cold grass at midnight, pointing out constellations. I remember his breath on my neck as I lay awake all night, worrying what it would be like after he was gone, my beautiful Mexican theater student with whom I briefly, and perhaps forever, fell in love.

THE POOLS OF PARADISE

David Holly

The rain had been falling for five days. Chill gusts buffeted me as I pedaled from my final college class of the day toward my house on Alder Street. Bicycling across the bridge, I had fantasized about a yummy guy in my American Literature class, but the cold driving rain rapidly turned my prospects toward a warm bath and hot sugared cocoa. Road muck splattered my pants legs, and my vision blurred from the rainwater running into my eyes.

A city bus approached from behind, crowding the bike lane as usual. I was muttering imprecations at the belligerent bus driver when I heard the crack of a water-laden limb above giving way. I gripped my brakes until they screeched, but I didn't have a chance. The limb stuck my right shoulder, knocking me from my bicycle. I tried to free my leg as I toppled sideways, but my bike frame forced me under the bus. The last thing I saw was a gigantic rear wheel rolling inexorably toward me.

* * *

Fewer than a dozen fellows reclined on roomy seats, which were covered with luxurious material. We were zipping along in an aerial craft unlike any airplane I'd encountered before. There was no air turbulence, no signs demanding we fasten our safety belts, and no flight attendants. Large round windows gave upon a blissful blue sky punctuated with charming puffs of pinkish cloud. The clouds dropped past our windows as if we were traveling straight up.

Not only was the scene appealing, my fellow passengers were gorgeous. As I looked around, I noticed that every guy was perhaps eighteen to twenty, fresh faced, hunky but not yucky-macho, and sweet smelling. We were dressed alike in shimmering white shorts and tops.

The guy across the aisle was smiling at me, so I smiled back. As my eyes traveled downward, I could see that he was sporting quite a significant boner. I promptly switched seats so that I was next to him.

"Hi, I'm Brandon," I said.

"I'm James."

Suddenly our introductions sounded like a bad cliché. The experience had such an air of unreality about it that I was hardly surprised at what happened next. James touched the tip of his swollen dick through the fabric of his shorts.

"It got hard when I saw you."

"No kidding?" I ventured, feeling like the idiot character in a poorly written porno flick. I had to be home, asleep, dreaming, and humping my pillow.

James started rubbing his dick through his sexy shorts. Nervously, I looked around to see if our fellow passengers were watching. I wanted to stroke James's dick too, but our position seemed frightfully public.

"Nobody will mind," James said, observing my hesitation. "In fact, you could slip off your shorts and sit on it, were you so minded."

Okay, that was just *too* fucking weird. "Are we joining the Mile High Club or something?" I asked as a flush of excitement shot through me. A natural bottom, I really wanted to sit on his cock. I felt my own cock hardening, and James grinned to see how much his suggestion excited me.

"Like, won't we get thrown off this...this thing?" I didn't know what to call our extraordinary shuttle.

"Nobody will mind," James repeated. "Come on. It'll be fun." He pushed down his shorts and I saw his thick, slightly brownish, circumcised penis directly. It looked like a bit of heaven.

All my life, I had gone for safer sex. I'd studiously demanded double condoms, yet I somehow knew that taking James's cock into my ass and receiving his come posed no danger to me. I had never felt so safe before, and I knew that I was going to do it. I was going to ride him bareback.

Hesitating no longer, I jumped up, pulled off my shorts, and grasped the head of James's dick. It was already slick with some lubricant, and at my touch, he leaked a pearly stream of spunk out his peehole. The juice ran across my hand. James caught my semen-wet hand, brought it to his mouth, and licked it clean. The action was so loving and so intimate that I nearly came on the spot.

For a moment, I wobbled, but I recovered whatever senses I still possessed, pulled my muscled asscheeks apart, positioned my asshole directly over James's cock, and slowly lowered myself upon him. My asshole opened readily as his cock slid into me. It was the most comfortable and natural penetration I had ever experienced. As I slid down toward his lap, he filled me deeply. There was not a hint of pain; indeed, the impaling was incredibly satisfying.

I found it easy to bounce upon James's cock. My muscles naturally carried me upward until his cockhead widened my anal sphincter, but before it pulled out all the way, I would slide downward, filling my ass repeatedly. As I rode, my own cock grew harder and pulsed with a fury for release. When I touched my cockhead, an electric tingle shot through me. Slowly I rubbed my cock as I rode James's dick.

James saw that I was masturbating my dry dick. "Let me, Brandon," he urged. "Let me jerk you off."

He reached around my waist with his strong right hand and touched the tip of my cock. From somewhere he had found a slick, warm lubricant that let his hand glide over my dick. The touch of his fingers and palm was like a soft kiss on my skin, yet his grip bit deep into my shaft and worked my cockhead like a tight squeeze.

"Oh, James," I murmured, hardly able to hold out for a moment. I had not realized how close I was to shooting my load until his hand began to massage my dick.

"Let it come, Brandon," James urged, his voice almost breathless in my ear as his hand plunged wildly upon my cock and I bounced just as wildly upon his. "I'm just about to come in your ass."

Rapturous tingles tortured my dickhead. "Oh, here I go," I moaned.

"I'm coming too," James declared loud enough for all the guys to hear. A guy in the seat in front of me turned around, watched me bouncing on James's cock, and smiled broadly.

"Isn't that one heavenly ride?" he quipped even as the first blast of come shot out of my cock. I knew that James was shooting his own spunk into me, which made me work all the harder at his cock with my asshole. I was milking him off with my anal sphincter even as his hand was milking my come.

* * *

I walked down a whispering rush-floored corridor hung with French tapestries, toward a door embellished with ornamental jade. Fearlessly, I turned the knob that felt so true in my hand. The office was roomy, yet a single sixteenth-century Persian carpet depicting flowering trees and animals covered the floor. One wall was a library of rare books done in fine bindings. The carpet was occupied by furnishings in a variety of styles. I recognized a pagoda cabinet with chinoiserie decoration, a French provincial sofa, and a Bernard van Riesenburgh table.

The stained glass window by Louis Comfort Tiffany depicted an idyllic lake with trees and birds; the window, which stood open in the perfect weather, gave upon an English garden. Elaborate fountain displays in the sixteenth-century style shot sprays that made music and their mist caught the sunlight to form rainbows above the lawn of Kentucky bluegrass. In the distance stood a pristine forest, and beyond the Alpine conifers, lofty snow-capped mountains rose toward the transcendent sky.

At the far end of the room stood a Chippendale library table, and behind it sat a beautiful young man, who arose upon my entrance. He smiled broadly and held out his arms to embrace me.

"Brandon," he said in dulcet tones. "You're here at last."

I knew that I had never seen him before, though he was acting as if I was a long-lost lover. Still, he was gorgeous, and I would have dropped to my knees without too much begging on his part. However, one compartment of my mind questioned what was happening. Events seemed to be following a dreamlike pattern, yet the details were too consistent to be dream wraiths. Outside the window, the landscape remained the same. The office did not suddenly shift into a roller coaster or a group fuckfest in the local bathhouse as usually happened in my dreams.

I was still dressed in the glistening white shorts and shirt, though the last time I'd thought about those shorts, they'd been draped around my ankles while my ass had been impaled by James's cock. For a second, I wondered whether I had imagined bouncing bareback on James's spurting cockhead. Yet the evidence was there. As my attention focused upon my crotch, I knew that I'd been fucked recently. My dick felt like it had been jacked, and my asshole was sticky. I still carried James's semen in my ass.

"Welcome, again, Brandon," my host greeted me. "I am Perdikoim."

Perdikoim wasn't the name of anybody I'd ever known, nor any guy I'd ever blown. The thought crossed my mind that I should have a bad feeling about the whole adventure, but I did not. I felt wonderful. I'd just had the best sex ever, and I was feeling healthy and happy. In fact, I'd never felt quite so good before. I had the strongest feeling that, whatever the situation, nothing bad was going to happen.

Perdikoim waved his hand toward a Hepplewhite armchair. Beside the chair was a Dolphin center-table with some papers and a Lithyalin glass beaker sitting upon its inlaid marble top. I took the seat he had offered and looked at the beaker. I had once seen a photograph of it in a book about antiques; in fact, every item in the room was a rare prize that I had seen in books and lusted after. The marbled glass held purplish liquor. Beside the glass, a Paul de Lamerie silver plate held little white cakes with pink rose frosting.

"Please, refresh yourself," Perdikoim urged.

I sipped the liquor and found it pure nectar. It was flavored with cherry and plum and mildly narcotic, yet it quenched the thirst marvelously. I sampled one of the cakes. It was pleasantly fruitful and sweet and slaked my hunger.

"A lost friend has been awaiting you, Brandon," Perdikoim said when I had eaten and drunk. "Shall we invite him in?"

"Sure." I was ready for a few answers, and I hoped this friend could provide them.

Perdikoim opened a side door and in rushed a young tuxedo cat, black and white, distinctively marked, and overjoyed to see me. He ran across the office, rubbed against my legs while meowing with a familiar tone, and leaped into my lap.

"Munchie," I exclaimed. I scratched Munchie behind his ears the way he always loved so much.

I must have had a heart, for it was beating loudly and quite fast. Munchie curled up in my lap, snuggled against my stomach, purred at full volume for a minute, and fell asleep. He was just the way I remembered him when he was young, except I also clearly recalled the day Munchie died from old age.

The truth that I had been suspecting for some time was borne upon me. I looked Perdikoim frankly in the eye and asked, "What are you, Perdikoim?"

"I'm an angel."

"I suspected as much," I huffed. "I got run over by a bus, didn't I? Did it kill me?"

Perdikoim made a face and perched upon the French provincial sofa. "Brandon, we don't use words like *kill, dead, death,* and their like. They're taboo words—the obscenities of this place."

"Well, how do you talk about 'you know what'?" I asked. Munchie awoke with another loud purr.

"No one needs to talk about it. You're past all that nonsense now. You suffered the 'grisly terror' and discovered that you are awake afterward."

For some reason, I did not feel the least grief over the occasion of my death. Munchie continued to purr, shifted his position so that his hind legs were digging into my stomach, and went back to sleep. "So this is Heaven?" I asked, glancing around the office.

Perdikoim laughed merrily at the question. "Not quite yet. You're on your way to your destination and this is a rest stop. By the way, I observed that you enjoyed your trip up."

Ah, yes, the trip up. If anything was going to determine my final destination, having gay anal intercourse on the way to Heaven was certain to have an effect. Yet, I felt a calm serenity, and Munchie continued to purr happily in his sleep.

"Perhaps there's something I should tell you..." I began, but Perdikoim interrupted me.

"No need. I know everything about you. I even know which Heaven you will choose, but the choice is still yours to make."

"I get to choose my own Heaven?" I started a bit at the novel idea. Munchie awoke again at my sudden jerk, gave me an offended look, and leaped to the carpet. I absently picked up a sheet of paper, crumpled it into a ball, and threw it across the room. Munchie raced after it, kicked it with his hind legs, and shredded it. In life, he and I had often played that old game.

"You get to choose," Perdikoim assured me.

"Where are my parents?" I asked. My family had been wiped out several years earlier when an airliner filled with evangelical Christians crashed on the way to a national political convention.

Perdikoim pulled another face. "They went to Evangelical Heaven," he said. "Behold."

Abruptly the far wall swirled into action until it became like a gigantic three-dimensional movie screen. I saw multitudes clad in white gowns praising a Deity who sat upon a white throne, and the fundamentalists never ceased to shout their hallelujahs and sing His praise. As I watched, a woman paused to catch her breath. Immediately, a cruel golden lash struck her across the back. The six-winged angel continued to lash her pitilessly until she had raised her voice in accord with the hosanna chorus. I could not imagine a situation that better suited my parents' theology.

"Holy crap!" I yelped.

"My sentiments exactly," Perdikoim assured me. "I know that you are destined for a better place."

"What do you have to offer?"

Perdikoim pointed toward the wall again, but this time it did not show one of the Heavens. It showed *me* on the trip up. In glorious three-dimensional color, I pulled off my shorts and positioned my ass over James's cock. I watched as I rode James's dick. Every motion was visible from every possible angle, and every sound was magnified. I could hear my own soft whimpers as I came close to orgasm.

Should I have felt ashamed, embarrassed, abashed, or guilty? Truth to tell, I enjoyed watching myself getting fucked almost as much as I enjoyed doing it. My cock hardened again, and I felt a pulsing arousal throughout my body. Perdikoim watched the action with a secret smile playing across his face. Even Munchie watched. My cat had witnessed similar scenes during his lifetime and even tried to join the action.

"Is there a place for me in Heaven?" I asked.

"Of course there is. Gay Heaven."

"Are cats allowed?"

"Certainly. Gay Heaven would be a poor place without cats. Take a look."

The scene on the wall shifted. A group of beautiful guys wearing bicycle garb, which fit their curves deliciously, were pedaling down a paved country path. The bushes were blooming brightly and the song of birds filled the air.

"They have bicycles in Gay Heaven?"

"Sure. Some guys bicycle there and some don't. Some just like wearing tight pants. Others like wearing no pants."

The scene shifted to a beach where a bunch of naked guys were tanning on the sand or playing some grab-ass game in the surf. The game appeared to involve numerous acts of gay sex, the winners or losers putting forth anally or orally as the rules demanded while the onlookers applauded.

Then we looked into a luxury suite where I was sitting with Munchie. I was reading aloud from a first edition of the Burton *Book of the Thousand Nights and a Night*, and my cat was listening attentively. Another man was with me, gazing fondly at me as I read, and a sexy male angel was serving frozen chocolate-banana daiquiris.

"A glimpse of your own future," Perdikoim commented. "Do you need to see more?"

I stooped and picked up Munchie. Holding my cat in my arms, I told Perdikoim, "That's the Heaven for me. Munchie and I are ready."

The sun shines large and warm in a sky of perfect blue. The refreshing breeze, which ripples the multicolored petals of the bougainvillea and rustles the broad-leafed orchids, wafts across me with the scent of jasmine. The swimming pool is crowded with hot-looking bikinis, swim briefs, and thongs into which even hotter-looking guys are stuffed. I stand on the ledge, admiring my own reflection, framed between the coconut palm fronds and the profusely flowering hibiscus. I am exquisite in my white swim briefs. I love my eternal body, just as we gay boys love to show off in swimsuits.

I dive headfirst into the pure water, creating hardly a splash as I cut through the surface. I float up next to Richard, who is resplendent in his hot-pink bikini with the tight seam up his crack. I met Richard soon after Munchie and I arrived in the gay paradise, and we have been lovers for millennia—if time has meaning.

Gripping Richard's solid buns, I kiss his lips until we descend toward the heavenly tiles on the bottom. Nobody drowns in Heaven, so we sink to an erotic mosaic of beautiful boys pleasuring one another. Hardly needing the enticement of the mosaic, I finger Richard's dickhead through the slick fabric of his bikini. Richard holds my ass with one hand while he fondles my dick with his other.

Within a minute, I have one hand down in Richard's swim briefs, and he gets his hand into mine. My dick is solid, so hard that it strains the front of my swimsuit. Richard is stroking my shaft, fingering my dickhead, and revolving his hand as if he is trying to unscrew a bottle cap. My right hand is busy in his swimwear, while my left hand slowly strokes his buttocks through the thin cloth made translucent by the water. My white swim briefs are transparent when wet.

Above our heads, guys are swimming, and the flashes of their tanned bodies and colorful swimsuits enhance the magic of the moment. We cannot talk beneath the surface, but we can feel each other's emotions. My heart races as I feel Richard's body moving through the stages of high arousal to approaching orgasm and ejaculation.

His nearness to coming rushes me to the edge. I feel my heavenly heart beating faster, my nostrils flaring, my nipples crinkling, my asshole contracting. On Earth, Renaissance wits dubbed orgasm the "little death." In Heaven, it is the "immense life." I work the head of Richard's cock with my thumb and forefinger, massaging it deeply, twisting and wringing it until I feel the ripples of rapture growing. I stroke hard again, striking his dickhead with my fist on each upstroke.

Richard follows suit, treating my cock as I treat his. My own ripples of pleasure are growing toward the *immense life*; throbbing waves wash down my cock, and my whole body stiffens. For a moment, all I can move is the pounding fist with which I beat Richard's meat.

Oh, Brandon, you're making me come, Richard thinks, his red fiery thoughts pure blasts of pleasure. Every guy in the pool feels the shock waves of our lust and emergent orgasms. Thunderous vortices of pleasure claim me; my body thrills to the rising blast. Richard's buns beneath my left hand tighten harder, grow rounder and more enticing (were an increase in perfection possible), and his muscles pump his first blast of come into his bikini.

My own jism flings forth in the next instant. Richard's cock discharges and gushes in my hand while my cock blasts its juices into his. Richard's face is a mask of unrestrained joy. Feeling the beams of my own visage, I kiss his lips as we linger in orgasm, rampage in ejaculation, and savor the fruits of the "immense life."

As our orgasms still, we slowly rise to the surface. "That was hot," Richard murmurs when our heads are clear of the water. He looks at Munchie, who has caught a mouse and is eating it fastidiously. Within minutes, the mouse will regenerate into a new body so it can go on with its mousy existence. Like the ripe fruit that we pluck from the trees, only to see it promptly replaced, nothing ends in Heaven.

"Let's cool off in the snow," Richard suggests.

No sooner has the image filled our minds than we are standing above the timberline on a snow-capped mountain. Our swimwear has been replaced by sexy, colorful winter costumes. We inhabitants of Heaven never need transportation. Once we visualize any place, we are there. The same goes for changes of clothing. A guy can follow the Earthly process, but Eternity can dispense with the productions of time. Richard and I bypass those mundane transitions.

Cooling from our exuberant orgasm, Richard and I snow-shoe through the winter fairyland, where the falling flakes make fantastic arabesques of the bushes and trees, while red and blue snow birds eat the honey sticks hanging from the spruce. When we tire, we snowshoe to a delightful Swiss chalet, where we slurp hot cocoa with shots of buttered rum and gorge on dark chocolate cake in twelve layers held with thick frosting and crèmes.

Back at the swimming pool, I call for Munchie. My cat has spent the afternoon chasing mice and butterflies, lapping cream from a glazed bowl, and napping under the croton bushes. He hurries to me, and we return to our apartment along the tern-roosting shore of a wide silver lake.

Our local newspaper, *The Elysian Gazette*, is filled with news of who has arrived in Gay Heaven that day and who has formed new friendships or found new lovers. Our personal angel, Sachiel, spreads a couple of pages of that day's *Gazette* onto the kitchen floor, scoops heated and boned mouse meat and songbird into an Irish blue glass dish, and gives this collation to Munchie, along with a fresh bowl of celestial water.

For Richard and me, Sachiel has prepared an equally scrumptious dinner: shredded chicken marinated in white wine and topped with fried noodles, mixed peas with shallots, potatoes baked in sea salt with cheese, bacon, and cream inside, green salad with Roquefort dressing, and ice cream topped with plum cordial and cocoa chunks.

Sachiel, who is delighted to play our flunky and cater to our every whim, is pretty scrumptious himself. Richard claims that Sachiel has more curves than a London playhouse. What

Richard means by that allusion I cannot say; his Earthly life occurred in an earlier time than mine, and in another country. Both Richard and I paddle Sachiel's round ass as he serves us, making the pretty angel giggle.

I have heard that in some of the Heavens, people do not eat or sleep; in some they don't even recognize each other, and there are no cats, bicycles, or books, not to mention cute guys in sexy sportswear. Not one of those places sounds like Heaven to me. Our Heaven, which Perdikoim deemed "Gay Heaven," is truly heavenly, and not only because gay guys desire it. In this happiest of Heavens, we eat, sleep, love, travel, and play.

At the end of another perfect day, Richard and I cuddle in our bed, ready to rest after our adventures and games, yet not quite ready for sleep. Richard's thick cock is hard before we ever hit the sheets. Since he is a natural top and I am an everlasting bottom, our relationship is perfect. I roll onto my stomach and pull up my right leg to give him easy access. Richard lubricates his cock and slips two slick fingers into my ass. I sigh with contentment as he pushes them into me. My cock is hard with lust as Richard prepares my asshole for action.

"You know, back in 1624, I got hanged for doing this very thing," Richard says with a laugh. "Publicly executed for buggering a cabin boy."

"People were *so* enlightened on Earth," I quip sarcastically. "Things weren't that great yet, even during my lifetime."

"None of that matters now." Richard climbs onto me and positions his slick cock against my hole. I push my anal sphincter to let him in. "That's why this is Heaven," he says, gliding delightfully into me.

As Richard slowly fucks me, Sachiel enters, smiles at our pleasurable activity, and lights scented candles, well placed where Munchie cannot brush against them. While Richard continues to fuck me, his heavenly tingles growing toward the long, sustained orgasm that will fire my own orgasmic delights, Munchie jumps onto the foot of our bed, watches with his feline eyes, and then curls into a ball to sleep the sleep of paradise.

As our orgasms climb, mounting minute by minute to greater heights of intensity, Sachiel whispers, "Good night, boys," and softly closes the door.

CHIAROSCURO

Jay Mandal

At this time of day, the ornate pump on its circular stone base was in shadow, as was the palm tree to its left. The lower part of the village hall was also in the shade, but the top was in the sun, along with the bell tower and the church. Light and dark, sun and shade. Chiaroscuro.

It was a view he never tired of looking at. But for how much longer would he be able to see it?

They'd come here in 1965 and had fallen in love with the place. Even when the law in Britain changed, they'd not returned. The people accepted them, welcomed them, even.

The square had been different then. The pump didn't work, so they had repaired it. No one seemed to care about the plants, so they had weeded and watered the soil, and watched as the garden flourished. And the people watched them. So what if they were both men? That was life.

Michael learned the skills necessary to survive in a small

community. Carpentry and joinery; painting and decorating; cleaning windows and mending shutters. Peter, usually a shy person, began to teach English in the school and to anyone who wished to learn. The women practiced as they sewed, their menfolk not jealous of the attention they paid to another man.

As the years passed, they absorbed the language, customs, and culture of the people. The local children—now fluent in English—grew up and had children of their own. Michael and Peter were asked several times to be godparents.

"But we're Protestant," they had objected at first.

"Who gives a fig?"

"The priest, for one."

"You let me talk to him."

"And we're—"

Antonio cut him off angrily. "You are good people. Who better to be godparents?"

One day, Michael caught sight of their reflections, and realized they'd grown old. Where had the time gone? When had their hair turned gray, their shoulders begun to curve, and their skin become fine like parchment?

Peter, as if he sensed something was wrong, looked up. "Yes?"

"I love you."

"Then I have everything I've ever needed or wanted."

"Don't leave me," Michael whispered.

"I shall never leave you."

They lost weight. Peter began coughing.

"A summer chill," he said. They both felt the cold now.

It didn't get better.

"See a doctor," Michael begged. But he knew how Peter hated hospitals and wasn't surprised when he refused. They were old, they had to accept these things.

Then one day, Peter coughed up blood.

Events moved swiftly after this. They saw a doctor—not the one in the village, but one at the hospital in the nearby town—who asked if Peter could come in for tests.

"Of course," Michael said immediately, overruling Peter. He felt guilty for not having realized Peter was ill, not simply old.

Peter remained in the hospital for a week. The tests came back. The doctor said he was very sorry. There was nothing more he could do.

"I want to die at home," said Peter, clasping Michael's hand in an unprecedented show of public affection.

"I'm not sure you're up to the journey to England."

"Not England. Home."

"All these people…" Michael indicated the villagers gathered around Peter's grave.

"It is too much?"

"No, it's wonderful. Thank you, Antonio."

Antonio squeezed his shoulder.

The new priest—the old one had passed away—looked at Michael. "Faith, hope, and charity," he said, speaking in his precise English. "But the greatest of these is charity." Another word for love.

The half-forgotten words brought tears to Michael's eyes.

When Michael next went for his daily walk, he hesitated at the point where the path forked. He and Peter would usually take the easier route to the right. Today he headed left in the opposite direction toward the village's small cemetery. He stood by Peter's grave for a few minutes, then he went and sat on the nearby bench in the pale, winter sunshine.

The days grew longer as winter gave way to spring. One morning, as he returned from the cemetery, Michael saw an easel had been set up in the square. In front of it stood a young man. Michael was curious but did not wish to disturb the stranger.

The young man was there again the next day when Michael returned home from his walk, and for several days afterward. They began nodding at each other.

Michael hurried back. If he was lucky, he'd escape the rain. The painter was in the square, seemingly oblivious to the darkening skies. Suddenly, there was a clap of thunder, and the boy looked up in dismay. He gathered up his brushes and paints and began struggling with the easel.

Michael knew the young man would never make it back to his lodgings before the heavens opened.

"This way," he said, taking the easel from the boy's hands. He led the lad into his house, and into the small sitting room. "Just in time!" Michael said, as the rain started to lash the window.

The boy shook his head, and rainwater flew everywhere.

"A towel," Michael suggested, and went off to get one. When he returned, he said: "And some soup. I always have soup after my walk if I'm not too tired."

The young man looked worried. "Please don't go to any trouble on my account."

"It's no trouble at all. I don't get many visitors nowadays." He turned on the gas, then began to get out bowls and spoons, and to cut bread. Soon the aroma of soup filled the room.

The boy wolfed down his food before Michael had barely

started his own. He must have been starving. No, he was simply young. Michael smiled.

A look of mortification crossed the young man's face. "I've eaten all the soup—"

"I have enough."

"I don't even know your name."

"Michael."

"I'm Daniel," the boy said, and they shook hands.

"How's your painting coming along?"

"Pretty well. I'll show it to you later. Of course, it's not quite finished." He hesitated. "That's if you'd like to see it."

"I'd be delighted to. Though my eyesight isn't what it used to be."

The young man carefully took out the picture.

Michael put on his glasses. Even he could see that the colors had been captured perfectly. He could almost feel the warmth of the sun on the stones.

"It's excellent," he said.

The boy relaxed, as if Michael's opinion was important to him.

They chatted while the rain continued to fall. Daniel had taken a year off from his studies to go around Europe but had been captivated by the village. He painted during the day and, in the evening, helped out in the bar.

During the following days, the weather reverted to its usual balmy state. Michael would go for his walk and on his return invite Daniel to share some soup or a cold drink.

They talked. Daniel told Michael about his home and his hopes of becoming a professional painter. Michael was more reticent but, after prompting from Daniel, told him about Peter. He even found a photo from their days at university together.

Michael could hardly make out Peter's face now his eyesight was so poor. He blinked.

"I'm sorry—I've upset you," Daniel said.

"It's my eyes. My father went blind and I'm losing my sight, too." Realizing that his candor had distressed Daniel, he changed the subject.

"It's finished!" Daniel announced one day as Michael returned from visiting Peter's grave.

"May I see it?"

"It's being framed."

Michael felt a dull ache of melancholy. The boy would surely be leaving soon. "Will you still be here for the harvest?"

"Antonio's talked me into it. He's got me down for treading the grapes. He said he didn't want me to damage my hands!"

They laughed.

"He was telling me that the harvest suppers have hardly changed since he was a boy. In the evening, everyone eats and drinks and then makes love in the open air." Daniel caught sight of Michael's face. "I'm sorry I didn't mean to remind you—"

"It's all right. We used to make love here. We never dared to outside." Michael remembered the warmth and dark, their two bodies entwined. They'd been so young, so full of hope.

The harvest supper wasn't the only thing Daniel and Antonio had discussed, as Michael found out a few days later.

"Please!" Daniel begged.

"A hospital?" Michael frowned. "Shouldn't you have asked me first?"

"We looked it up on the Internet. You aren't going blind. Medicine has moved on since your father's day. They can cure you."

"They didn't cure Peter."

Antonio intervened. "Peter's gone," he said gently. "It was too late to save him. Do you think he'd want you to suffer in order to expiate your feelings of guilt that he died and you're still alive?"

Michael sank wearily into his battered old armchair. Antonio was right, of course. There'd been a time, just after Peter's death, when Michael thought he had nothing to live for. No wonder he'd accepted his deteriorating eyesight without question.

"All right," he said.

"The car will be here tomorrow."

"I need to pack."

"Maria will help."

At last the day of the harvest supper arrived. There were toasts to the crop, the village, and God. People congratulated Michael on his "miracle cure," and said their good-byes to Daniel, who was leaving the following day.

"Come and see me before you go," Michael said, his hands resting lightly on Daniel's shoulders.

"Of course I will. How could I leave without saying good-bye properly? Or even improperly!" He gave an impish grin, and then added: "Thank you."

"Whatever for?"

"You've cooked me soup, and taught me about love."

"But you gave me back my sight. Let's call it quits."

"Come on, you two! Don't look so serious. This is meant to be a party." Antonio turned to Daniel. "There're lots of pretty, young girls wanting to dance. What are you waiting for?"

Daniel grinned and excused himself.

"You'll miss him. I'll miss him," said Antonio. They watched as Daniel whirled around the makeshift dance floor. "And the girls will certainly miss him." They both laughed. "Here, have some more wine."

The next day, Michael didn't go for his usual walk. Not only was he afraid of not seeing Daniel, but his head ached. A hangover at his age! A pity to pass up his visit to the cemetery, but Peter would understand.

A knock came at the door.

Daniel stood there, looking shy but apparently none the worse for the previous night's celebrations.

There was some small talk, which dried up quickly as neither knew quite what to say.

Daniel broke the silence. "Well, I suppose…"

"Wait! I have something to give you." Michael picked up a box from the table and gave it to the boy.

"I have a present for you, too." Daniel handed him a parcel. "I did two paintings."

"Two?" Michael unwrapped the brown paper.

"They said you mended the pump."

The picture showed two figures working in the square.

"I copied one of your photos," Daniel added.

Tears welled up in Michael eyes. Old man's tears.

"You don't like it."

"Of course I like it. How could I not like it? Thank you, Daniel." Michael paused. "Peter said he'd never leave me, but some promises you can't keep. I wish you could have met him."

"So do I. He was a lucky man."

Michael looked up, surprised.

"He had you."

"We had each other."

Daniel glanced at his watch.

"Don't forget your present," Michael said, his voice suspiciously gruff.

"Can I open it now?" Daniel undid one end. "An easel!"

"A *folding* easel," Michael amended. "I thought it might come in handy."

"I'll take care of it," Daniel promised.

"Never mind the easel, just take care of yourself."

"That goes for you, too."

The two men stood looking at each other.

They heard a car door slam, followed by Antonio's voice.

"Antonio's here with the car. I've got to go. Thank you for everything."

They embraced.

"Good luck," Michael said.

Michael shivered. He fetched a pullover from the bedroom, and sat down in the old armchair. With the arms of Peter's sweater wrapped around him, he was soon fast asleep.

AS SWEET BY ANY OTHER NAME

Mark G. Harris

Ralph, a ticklish young dodger with no carpentry skills, had been coerced into helping renovate a tree house. The hulking oak that cradled the tree house had sprouted, generations before, in the dividing line between two properties down the street from where Ralph lived. Therefore, like all trees, it belonged to no one.

Neither household on either side of the tree claimed it. They did not dispute the tree house in its boughs, considering it, as well, public property. This surprised nobody. The street, protected underneath umbrellas of elm and the aforementioned oak, was a civil and merry place where the houses were shingled and aged but, as the saying went, kept up.

Novembers found the cars on either side of the drizzled street parallel-nestled under the interlaced limbs, with wet orange and red leaves stuck to their bumper stickers, stickers that promoted political hopefuls or urged peeling messages of world peace. In high blooming Aprils, from the open windows of the nearby piano instructor, dusty and forgotten composers found students to cherish and remember them, if in a plodding but always improving way, beneath the branches' breeze-tickled sway.

The street and its mellow inhabitants, human and arboreal, had charmed Ralph, lured him into taking an apartment there, and provided a golden sense of comfort after the smarting breakup with his boyfriend Nick, on whom Ralph had finally begun to stop dwelling, as he persisted in telling himself.

And then Ralph told himself, "Three fifty-two? Can it really be that late?" as he dropped the paperback of poems by Yeats on his lamplit side table and answered the soft knock at his door.

Yolanda, a neighbor from the house next door, stood in the upper stairwell outside Ralph's apartment. In her left hand she gripped the box wrench she had borrowed from him six months ago. "Why are you still awake?"

"The better to answer the door. And, hi. I let my bedtime get away from me, I guess. And I bought myself a new wrench four months ago, so you might as well keep that one. Want to come in?"

She pocketed the tool in her red rickrack-trimmed apron and made herself at home on Ralph's only chair, while he returned to his spot on the sofa. She fussed with her dreads and brought up the topic of the tree house.

The tree house, handsome, overgrown, roofed, and rambling, was quite complete. However, in that neighborhood it was tradition to add to the tree house when anyone on the street delivered a baby. In this case the neighbors were organizing, the coming weekend, to build a turret. The addition was in honor of wee healthy Pablo John Jenkins, born a week before at Number 16, the house with the elaborate scrollwork that, in a less agreeable neighborhood, would inspire bitter envy among the neighboring houses rather than homey pride.

"Want to help us?" Yolanda said. "The pay sucks, meaning there isn't any, but I've noticed your weekends aren't exactly booked, anyway."

"How can anybody resist you?" He fondled his felt bookmark and then laughed. "You know, it's great that some woman had a baby and all, but if I were to run off and have some unprotected sex, I'd get a lecture, not a tree house. I swear, heterosexuals and their baby showers and other bizarre rituals."

"Did you just say something about you having sex? Dirty talk. How rare." Yolanda yawned. "All I ever get out of you, every Monday morning, is, 'Yeah, I stayed in this weekend and darned socks,' or something."

"Those darn socks."

"This has got to stop."

Unsure if she referred to his lame puns or his secluded convalescence, Ralph went with a neutral, "Really—and spoil the fun?"

"You owe me some sweaty man-on-man postgame commentary, or whatever it is you sports like to call it."

He smiled at her and admired her eyes for a second. "Maybe one of these days that'll happen to me again." Ralph, much like any other hopeful so named, wanted to favor, to be pleasant, and to mate.

Ralph would say, "Hear, hear," when in agreement. He would say, "There, there," when he sympathized. He would say, "Duran Duran," for that matter, if asked the performer of that long-ago song about a hungry wolf, if only to demonstrate how like any other Ralph to be found here or there he could be. His soft pulsing heart had entered the fray of men and emerged disfigured, but there no knight was safe, no matter how glorious or inauspicious was his dubbing.

The breakup with Nick had left tarnish on Ralph's armor.

Yolanda, a craftsperson by trade, had the sort of trained eye that could zero in on this sort of imperfection, and the urge that all friends have to want to remedy the situation. She mentioned the possibility of her available friend John showing up to lend a hand with construction of the tree house that weekend. She was cut off from divulging further details about John's history, eye color, or opinion of Shakespeare, this last a matter of vital importance to Ralph, when another set of knuckles rapped on Ralph's door.

Terry, Ralph's fellow-insomniac neighbor from across the hall, straight as an arrow and just as slender, soft-voiced a, "Can I come in? I heard talking," and was shown inside. Terry returned the cookie cutters borrowed from Ralph and sat on the floor near Yolanda's dusty crossed boots. Terry often dropped by for brief discussions late at night, but tended to stay longer when Yolanda happened to be present. Ralph suspected that Terry liked Yolanda.

He fetched two cold soda pops from his kitchen and set them between his neighbors who were, without knowing it, decorating his otherwise monastic living room. Ralph preferred to bedeck a room with friends instead of with knickknacks. He listened to them bicker.

"Correct me if I'm wrong," Yolanda said to Ralph, "but it's May. What is this airhead doing," her motor oil–stained finger indicated Terry, "borrowing cookie cutters from you when it's nowhere near Christmas?"

Ralph understood Terry's reticence in making an overture Yolanda's way, and it had nothing to do with Yolanda's propensity for the brusque. In his encounters with the single, the eligible, and the fascinating, Ralph, too, clammed up. He returned to his sofa, drew his cozy blanket around him, and, to the tune of their chatter, soon enough fell asleep. Ever since his breakup, silence and the lack of human noise had bothered Ralph, and he was glad to have found a solution tonight. He smiled, perhaps dreaming. His problem with meeting men could wait, but perchance there he was dreaming, too.

He was reminded of his problem late on Saturday afternoon, when he approached the tree house and located Yolanda amid the swarm of would-be carpenters. She accessed him.

"What are you wearing?" she said. He prided himself on having understood her despite the drywall screw clamped in the corner of her mouth, as if she had taken up smoking the hard stuff. "I go to all this trouble," she said, "fixing you up with one of my in-house stallions, and the best you can manage is a shirt that does zilch for you?"

He had forgotten about her friend John, the heart candidate. The week had been a stable one but the weekend, he saw, was turning into an emergency situation.

The shirt Ralph was wearing was uncomfortably fancy, one his old boyfriend Nick had given him. He wondered if a woman wearing a pair of overalls with a big rip in the ass and a SHAZAM! T-shirt was in the position to mete out fashion dictates, and decided, for what little he knew about the topic, that it was best not to argue. Ralph nodded and began walking back to his apartment, and his closet.

This had been a ridiculous idea, he told himself, this attempting to meet someone new and to risk his heart. His heart's neighbor, his stomach, was beginning to writhe and revolt, as if anticipating where the state of the neighborhood was going.

He paused on the sidewalk when he saw old Mrs. Jenkins in her wheelchair on the front porch of Number 16, surfing the Internet with one hand and rocking a basinet containing the inspiration for today's construction with the other. He envied the baby's sleep. "Hi, there, Mrs. Jenkins," he said. "That must be your new grandson, eh?"

"Oh, about the same as I always am," she said, squinting at Ralph in the leaf-dappled light. "I'd be better if Mr. Jenkins was still with us."

Ralph wasn't sure when Mrs. Jenkins had lost her husband, or lost her hearing, but the dull image of himself, lonely and bereft, now and in the years to come, haunted his imagination and shut out all other considerations. Did he want to remain alone? Did he want to say he had never tried to find somebody to love again? In his head, Yeats's "Brown Penny" began its opening whisper, which drowned out, with irony, all of Ralph's loud protests against new love.

The feeling that he was wasting what precious time he had been given shamed him, there in the shade, particularly when he happened to own a magic yellow-and-white baseball shirt. The shirt, given what the cut of it did for his shoulders and arms, and his self-esteem, might have made Ralph appear more appealing, and it was folded in his dresser, mere footsteps away, if only he could dredge up the derring-do to take those steps.

His old boyfriend Nick had never cared for that shirt, and had once belittled Ralph for wearing it, claiming its shabby condition caused Ralph to resemble something with B.O. in a bus depot.

Though he hadn't worn the shirt since that historic comment, Ralph could recall as if from yesterday how the shirt felt, sleepily soft, second-skin comfortable, priceless, and well worth the brown pennies the thrift store had charged him for the old thing. Only thus armored might Ralph steel himself to attempt knighthood again, and attempt to favor, to be pleasant, and to mate.

And to throw up, more than likely. He scrapped the idea.

And so he returned to the assortment of scrapped and salvaged woodwork that would be used for the tree house's addition, resolved to at least hammer one generous nail in tribute to Pablo John Jenkins, the Healthy and Wee, before running back home for safe cozy cover. Ralph comforted himself with the thought that, for centuries, chickening out had been a viable alternative. William Butler Yeats could go launch a kite.

Ralph spied a clean-cut, confident man talking to Yolanda. He overheard her call the man *John*. A chilly certainty plucked on his tight nerves that this man was the friend with whom Yolanda intended to shackle Ralph. This man, without meaning to, terrified Ralph. Guillotines were clean-cut and confident, too, if one looked and philosophized long enough.

In Ralph's mind men like this, or like his old boyfriend for example, never left the house without a close shave and a pressed shirt. Perhaps their league seemed to suspect that Casual Fridays were diabolical plots devised by the Salvation Army, or Old Navy, or some other branch of an informally dressed militia out for blood, or at the very least out for creases and worn knees.

Ralph had tried to keep up along that certain man's elegantly paved road before, and knew that he lacked the fuel to endure another attempt at it. He ducked out of view, behind two women who were carrying several long boards, and clambered up the tree house's ladder.

In the tree he found a young fellow hunkered down on the decking, with two wooden drumsticks in his hardy two fists, teaching a little boy how to drum.

"Oops—hi," Ralph said.

The fellow nodded without removing his gaze from his percussive task.

"Mind if I watch?" Ralph said. "I'm sort of hiding from someone."

"Sure." The fellow smiled, continuing the lesson.

Quite a different drummer, this one. His smile pleased Ralph in the same way that rivers enjoy moons reflected in their rippling. Working fast, Ralph pilfered an inventory of the fellow's pointed white canines, his convoluted chest hair curling around the collar of a gray T-shirt, and his long forearms, before the smile, and the lesson, ended.

"Sorry about that." The fellow offered his mild keen eyes, and an open hand to shake, to Ralph. "Anyway, hello. Friends call me Wolfie."

Ralph grasped his hand. "Mine call me Ishmael," he said, hoping for if not a laugh then at least another glimpse of that smile.

"Who are you hiding from?"

"Um." No clever story, at that instant, came to Ralph. "A guy my friend is setting me up on a date with," he said. "I just got a look at him—not my type, you know?"

"Aren't you supposed to be dating girls?" the little boy said.

"Hey, now. Aren't you supposed to eat your vegetables?" The fellow poked a finger in the boy's stomach, making him giggle. "You probably like brussels sprouts as much as he likes girls, so lay off."

Ralph sat, slid his legs between the mismatched balusters of the railing, and let his feet dangle and swing. "What I'm supposed to be doing," he said, "is helping to add to this tree house. I'm about as qualified to do that as I am to date somebody, though." He smiled. "But enough about me. What aren't you qualified to do?"

"How much time you got?"

"You seem pretty good with those sticks."

"Yeah." He sat next to Ralph and swung his feet, as well. "I mean, thanks. I'm working on it. I rent a studio, downtown. It's deserted there at night, no one to bother, good for practicing, you know? I mean, I get a little loud and crazy with it."

"We're still—" Ralph stopped himself from ending with, *talking about drumming, aren't we?* He chose to leave it at that, as if the statement were deep philosophy and not the result of sitting too close to the tense thighs of this lad, of begrudging the breeze that tugged on the frayed strings of his denim shorts.

"Where's this guy you're avoiding?"

Ralph pointed at the combed head of hair that was still bent in conversation with Yolanda's dreads. "There he is."

"Total ogre. Doesn't deserve you."

Ralph pressed his forehead against the rail, still looking at the man below in the way that snaggletoothed children look at orthodontists. "All right, all right. Maybe he's not so bad. I don't know. It's just, he's—what's the word? Fastidious?"

"Human?"

"He seems like the kind of guy who'd have a different shoe for each occasion. Does that make any sense?"

"I have a different shoe for each foot."

"He reminds me of my ex," Ralph said.

"Ah." For the span of a moment the swinging of their legs achieved rhythmic unison, and then fell back into their differing speeds. "My ex couldn't take my drumming at night. I keep hoping, though, and try not to let people with ears get me down."

Ralph stood, brushed off his backside, and sighed. "I guess I'm not giving him much of a chance, am I? Least I can do is say a quick, 'Hello,' and see what he's like."

Ralph's counsel stood, as well. "I need to get going, myself. I tell you, all this not working is making me hungry."

"Like the wolf?" Ralph performed a sting with his index fingers on the railing. "Sorry. I ought to leave the drumming to you."

"No, no, you're not bad, there. I see a bright future for you."
He offered Ralph his hand again. "Anyway, very nice meeting
you, Ralph. If you're free later, I'm meeting my bandmates
tonight, at Storky's. You know it?"

"Not sure. Wait, I think so. College crowd, dubious food,
dynamite jukebox?"

"There you go." As he descended from the tree house he
added, "And my friends don't really call me Wolfie. My ex used
to, though. He thought it fit me. My name's John."

"John?"

"Yeah, John. One of the many, the proud. Anyway, see you.
Hopefully."

"Why did you just call me Ralph? I didn't tell you what my
name is."

"That's right, Moby Dick, you didn't." The early evening
sky was blooming with the color of lemonade, as John walked
toward his old Volkswagen Beetle parked at the curb. He looked
back at Ralph and smiled.

Ralph called, "So, what do you think of Shakespeare?"

John made a face and swiveled his splayed level hand as if it
were the deck of a rocking boat. "He's no John Bonham," he
yelled, before getting into his car, starting it, and puttering away.

Something, some rewarding quality of the warm air, made
the starting night feel unfettered. Ralph's old boyfriend had
not cared much for Shakespeare either. Housed up among the
wriggling green oak leaves, Ralph closed his eyes and opened
them and made the reckoning to not let his old boyfriend hinder
him for one day more. Besides, John's bumper stickers agreed
with him.

"He called you a dick," the little boy said with glee, using
the drumsticks that John had left behind and employing Ralph's
right shin as a substitute snare drum.

"When he's right, he's right," Ralph said. "And, by the way, ouch."

As much as Ralph had figured that he would dread the experience of embarking from the tree house for solid ground, or coming back to earth, the act of it was not so bad. He smiled when he found Yolanda resting in the grass and eating one of the cookies that Ralph's insomniac neighbor Terry had made.

"Where'd that guy go," Ralph said to her, "that you were talking to?"

"I could ask you the same question, but my mouth's full."

"Doesn't seem to be stopping you any." Ralph sat next to her.

"So? What'd you think of John?" she said. "His space is downtown, next door to my workshop. Hot ass, huh?"

"And then some. And, hey, pretty thoughtful of Terry, bringing cookies, eh? Tree-shaped cookies, at that. Indeed, very thoughtful."

She glowered. "Don't start with me. I'm the matchmaker around here."

"He likes you."

"I know." Yolanda wiped her mouth on her T-shirt. "He? Oh, my god. I thought Terry was a lesbian."

"Easy mistake, I guess. He's a very pretty boy."

"Or a very butch girl," Yolanda said, "depending on the light."

"Poor guy. He probably thinks he doesn't stand a chance with you. I think he's got the idea that you're a lesbian, too."

"Now, see, everybody keeps saying that to me. I, for one, don't get that."

With the day's work at an end, Ralph linked his arm with Yolanda's while he walked her home, comparing notes on whether it was he or she who was the more clueless about lovers.

She invited him inside her house for a beer, but Ralph declined. He had sudden dinner plans and needed to change his shirt. He hummed while he did so. Foolish, same as love, though it might have been, a reverie had already found happy occupancy in his thoughts, one of drowsing on a bed while a drummer drummed nearby, under an inconstant moon, downtown.

FINDERS KEEPERS

Rob Rosen

Red-eyes, the very bane of my existence.

Careerwise, I was frequently required on both coasts, but I chose to live on the west one rather than the east. The weather was nicer, the men were hotter, and I'd take earthquakes over sleet anytime.

On that particular run, I was leaving on an almost-midnight flight, having to be in New York for an early morning meeting. Slogging through the airport, barely even aware of my surroundings, I'd come to the sad realization that the United terminal had become my veritable second home. Collapsing onto a too-hard seat, my briefcase toppling to the worn carpet, I stared downward and sighed.

It was then I spotted it: a shiny penny, faceup, brimming with good luck.

Superstition taking hold of me, I bent down to retrieve the auspicious object. Suddenly, my head, already foggy from lack of sleep, came crashing, *whammo*, into a surprisingly solid object.

When the stars stopped their clockwise spin, and with my hand rubbing my aching skull, I peeked through my squinting lids.

A man sat crouched on the ground in front of me, a smile on his face and the penny held firmly in his grasp. "Finders keepers," he proclaimed while rubbing his temple, wincing as he did so. "Sorry," he quickly added.

I laughed, despite the dull throbbing in my noggin. "Guess we both need all the luck we can get, huh?" I asked, standing up to offer him a hand, helping him back to his feet.

"Childhood habit," he replied, his grip tightening in mine, until we stood face-to-face, his dazzling blue eyes inches from mine, his breath smelling of cool peppermint.

"Same here," I said, my own breath growing instantly shallow as my heart began a beat-laden samba. "And sorry, as well."

The handshake kept going, moving in auto-repeat. Flesh on glorious flesh. Our eyes stayed open, locked, not a blink, not a shift up or down or to the side, laser-locked, neither wanting, it seemed, to break contact.

"Steve," he finally said, by way of introduction, his hand at last letting go, his eyes blinking once.

"Dan," said I, after a blink of my own. "So, where are you headed?"

He grinned again, revealing a bright, white smile that stretched across his impossibly handsome face. "Not headed. Arrived. From New York for a meeting in the morning. Yourself?"

"The same, only in reverse."

He laughed and then mock-frowned. "Guess that penny wasn't so lucky after all."

I gulped. He was flirting with me. My knees went weak, my breath turned ragged, and my arm suddenly ached to reach out and pull him in tight. I went for broke, upping the ante. "I don't know about that," I corrected. "Two ships, once passing in the night, now stem to stem. Seems lucky enough."

A red flush crept up his neck and bloomed on each stubbled cheek. "Do either one of these two ships have a bar on them? I could use a drink right about now."

"The ships, no. The United club room, yes. And my plane doesn't board for another thirty minutes. You *up* for it?" I offered, the double entendre gliding from my lips and hanging in mid-air.

He leaned in, his mouth moist against my ear. "Wanna see how up for it I am?"

We hurried to the club room, slamming both our membership cards *smack* on the table. "Um, shower room," I requested, practically panting.

"Two," he added, stifling a giggle.

The staff handed us towels and card keys, barely even noticing us. Midnight shifts are a bitch for everyone. In any case, we walked in double time to the rear of the club, entering one, not two, shower stalls.

"Let's put these ships into dry dock," he said, locking the fingers of both my hands with his and pushing me upright against the cool tile, his mouth instantly finding my own, pressing hard, harder still, as if his body ached to become one with mine.

When he let me up for air, I replied, "How about I dock my mouth on your ass?"

He grinned. "Great minds think alike."

He kicked off his shoes, as did I. Letting go of my hands, he deftly unbuttoned his dress shirt, then yanked it out of his slacks and off his body, revealing a slim, ripped torso, densely hairy with two rigid, eraser-tipped nipples poking through the fuzz. My own shirt was off in a jiff, followed quickly by my pants and boxers, and then just as quickly by his, until both of us stood in nothing but our socks, with hefty cocks that began their gradual lifts up, Up, UP.

"Nice," I rasped, twirling my finger in the air to indicate that I now wanted to see the flipside. He obliged, getting on all fours, his alabaster ass upturned, his cheeks spread apart, and a pink, crinkled hole winking up at me. He was hairy fore to aft, and just as yummy. I crouched, taking a deep whiff. "Damn, you smell good," I moaned.

"And taste even better," he amended.

I eagerly tested that theory, which did indeed prove to be fact. My tongue darted out, licking around and around, zeroing in on the sweet beckoning center before it delved inside his satin-smooth interior. He moaned and bucked his ass into my face, while I reached between his thighs to pull and yank and stroke his swollen cock, already slick with sticky precome.

"Best meal I've had all day," I said, in between sucks and slurps on his pink, perfect hole.

"What about me?" he asked. "I'm starving up here."

Only too happy to oblige, I slung my legs through his, serving up my cock to satiate his hunger. He downed it in one fell swoop, sending an eddy of adrenaline to my crotch that ricocheted through the length of my body. I, in turn, pulled his rod down and through, coaxing it inside my mouth and down my throat, while my spit-slick fingers worked their way deep within his ass.

He moaned softly and jacked my cock in between sucks, causing my balls to bounce in anticipation. "Close," I groaned, entrenching three digits inside his rump, up and back to the hilt. "Real close."

"Ditto," he agreed, his cock swelling to mammoth proportions, and his prostate hardening beneath my incessant prodding and pounding.

And then I shot, ounce after creamy, hot ounce, which I could hear hitting the tile beneath me as it exploded from my quivering cock. Aiming his prick over my shoulder, and with a final tug and then push up his ass, he came as well, sending a come-bath out against the floor and the wall. Our moans and groans and sighs filled the small enclosure, reverberating against all that smooth tile and echoing joyously in my ears.

Sadly, there was no postcoital aftermath, no warm glow to enjoy. The speakers outside the stall broke the spell, announcing the imminent departure of my plane.

"Shit," I said, hopping up, toweling off as best I could, and lickety-split getting redressed, while he sat there, naked and dripping, watching me with that glorious grin of his.

"Lucky fucking penny," he said with a wink as I bent down for one long, deep, wonderful kiss that ended all too soon.

"Oh, yeah," I agreed, pressing my lips firmly against his, etching the moment into my brain to be forever remembered, just before I rushed from the shower, outside the club, and onto my plane, mere moments before they irrevocably shut the door behind me.

My heart leapt into my throat and my stomach churned, realizing that I somehow already missed him, and knowing all too well that we hadn't exchanged anything but first names and copious amounts of bodily fluids.

Two ships that bumped and then did indeed pass in the night.

I fell asleep dreaming of him, about those eyes of his that now twinkled behind my own, blue as sapphires, lighting up the darkness. When I awoke, I was in the Big Apple, with a pit the size of a big lemon in my belly.

Fated to meet, fated to part, it felt like.

"Fuck," I groaned, and headed to my meeting, my lips buzzing at the fading memory of his lips, of his ass and cock on my mouth, of his hirsute body perched atop mine. "Fuck," I glumly repeated, resigned to winning and then promptly losing him.

The following weeks went by in a blur. Rather than forgetting him, my memories only grew more intense. Each trip to the airport and to the United club room, and each search for him therein, proved fruitless.

And then, just when I'd given up hope of ever seeing him again, there he was, miraculously exiting the plane I was soon to board. His eyes locked on to mine almost immediately, the familiar wide grin gleefully spreading across his adorable face. He walked up to me and gave me a hug, whispering in my ear as he did so, "Funny thing about ships, they tend to follow the same routes."

I laughed and held on tightly, taking in the heady aroma of him. "It's good to see you again, Steve," I whispered back. A gross understatement if ever there was one.

He sighed. "Ditto, Dan."

Then he reached into his pocket and held up the familiar penny for me to see. "Looks like the luck is holding out."

I smiled and drew him in even closer. "Except we're passing in the night again. No time to even dry-dock. The plane's late. They'll be boarding me too soon."

He looked me deep in the eyes, his shimmering like a perfect midday sky. The smile briefly faltered. "Is it, um, weird to say I missed you?"

"Try me," I replied.

He kissed me, softly and lushly, the crowd vanishing from my periphery, until only he and I remained. When his lips lifted from mine, he said, "Okay then, I missed you."

I laughed. "You're right. That was weird. Because I missed you, too."

And then it was his turn to laugh. "See, just like I told you before, great minds think alike." He paused in thought, his mind obviously racing, and then he added a hasty, "Wait right here."

Before I could say anything, he was off like a shot, racing down the concourse and out of sight. I grinned and waited, and waited some more as the grin slowly vanished and the lemon-sized pit gradually returned.

Soon enough, they started boarding the plane, and I could wait no longer. I looked up and down the concourse, but he was nowhere to be found. Gone again. Lost in the night. Unmoored and drifting, drifting away from me.

In profound dismay, I boarded the plane, taking my seat and resting my weary head against the cold, thick-paned window. I closed my eyes and again saw his, sparkling blue, beckoning me in like the ocean on a hot summer's day. It was all I could do to not sit there and cry.

"Penny for your thoughts," came the voice, rattling me out of my reverie.

When I opened my eyes, there he was, handing me the shiny coin and taking the seat next to mine, ready to make the return trip, only this time by my side.

I smiled and nodded. "What about finders keepers?" I asked, pocketing the penny and then placing my hand in his.

He leaned in and brushed his lips against mine. "Fine then, I found you and now I'm keeping you. Okay?"

I shrugged and kissed him long and deep. "Okay by me, but you live in New York and I live in San Francisco."

And then he laughed, squeezing my hand as he did so. "No, Dan. Both of our ships dock at the same port. We just seem to depart at different times, is all."

And then I laughed, resting my head against his, and again closing my eyes. "Thank goodness for red-eyes, Steve," I said to him.

"Amen to that, Dan. Amen to that."

KINDRED SOULS

Vic Bach

It was the start of an intense, long-term relationship, the start of love. Of course, neither Will nor I had any way of knowing it. We first met, awkwardly, in the nether regions of cyberspace. I had placed a personal ad in the *Blade*, headlined SEEKING KINDRED SOUL. (That's how earnest I am, despite my age and advanced education.) I was facing my sixties alone, yet fairly new to gay life. After a few episodic encounters, I was still seeking the male soulmate of my fantasies.

Will lived and worked in Belfast, in telecommunications, but yearned to experience New York. At the age of twenty-five, with a vacation in mind, he followed his impulse and booked an August flight and a two-week stay at a hostel he found on the Internet, in the Chelsea area—four to a room—at a price he could afford. His early email struck a valiant chord: *Nothing ventured, nothing gained.* My ad interested him, particularly the promise of *good conversation, so lacking in gay life.* He wondered if we might meet when he was in the city.

Just eighteen months before, I had moved into my own apartment—a rent-stabilized studio on West 77th Street opposite the museum—to live separately from my wife. The reasons were complicated and had little to do with sexual leanings or my long-deferred desire for male intimacy. After the move, I felt the aloneness and resolved to become close to another man for once in my life. The late shift in sexual identity was difficult, fumbling, and closeted, but it was accomplished. I joined several groups at the Center—the Gay, Lesbian, Bisexual, and Transgender Community Center. My few sexual encounters were physically fulfilling but emotionally bankrupt. The longest was three months of "going steady" with a fifty-year-old Brooklyn guy with whom I couldn't hold a decent conversation. When we parted I decided, for the first time, to place that ad.

I met with the more interesting respondents, one by one, and came up dry after a month of screening. Then I received an email response all the way from Ireland, from an articulate young man named William. I was puzzled and surprised; the power of telecommunication was new to me. The idea of meeting him struck me as absurd, given our vast differences in age and culture, and his transient stay in New York. Without answering, I filed the response away with the others in my locked office cabinet.

A week later, responses had dwindled to zero and I decided to shred the file. When I came upon William's note again, on sheer impulse I sent a short message back with my phone number, suggesting he call when he was in the city—we might meet for coffee or a drink. *Why not?* It might be an interesting, if brief, intercultural experience. I thought that would end it, but the note began a seductive, six-week correspondence of mounting intensity. We traded photos and several transatlantic phone calls, and planned to meet the day he arrived.

Given the ocean that parted Will and me, and our differences in age and background, we were not likely candidates to meet offline, even during his visit to the city. That summer of 2000 Manhattan was flush with postmillennial excitement. Tourists flooded the streets, hotels were booked solid, restaurants were more than their usual crowded and noisy. We might have met by chance, I suppose, in a bar, or maybe in Central Park, if I had the nerve for that kind of encounter. But it would have been unlikely.

It was Tuesday, August first. I made sure I was home to receive Will's call in the early evening, when he was scheduled to arrive at the hostel. All week I had labored to clean the apartment, clearing the layer of dust, scrubbing floors. Some last-minute tidying needed to be done. Then I folded the open futon into a respectable sofa and stowed the bedding in the closet. After I showered, with the phone nearby, I chose my black slacks because the effect was slimming. The weather was torrid—in the nineties, heavy with humidity. There would be no concealing jacket. Instead, I wore a cool purple, pin-striped shirt, sleeves rolled to mid-arm, and set aside a black shirt to take with me in case of rain. I was conscious of the care I was taking for a casual meeting that would go nowhere, with a young man who struck me as mousy in his email photo. Despite the ambivalence and the dread, I was also excited. It was, after all, a date.

Will's call came later than expected, after he had showered and changed. The subway ride down was quick, I had only a short walk south on Eighth Avenue to the hostel. At West 30th Street, I could see a young man leaning against the brick façade, waiting expectantly. He was boyish-looking, medium height and frame, with blond-brown hair reflecting the evening sun. I called "Will?" and he beamed at me. He had a pleasing, clean-shaven face; his smile was bright and open. The email photo did him no justice. He seemed happy to see me—there was no sign of disappointment.

As we shook hands I pressed my other hand warmly on his shoulder. "Well, at last we meet."

He smiled back. "Amazing, isn't it?"

I hailed a cab on the avenue. Once we were settled, I kicked off the conversation.

"Sorry about the traffic, and the weather is unbearable. You're not seeing the city at its best."

"Oh, no, it's wonderful to be here!" His enthusiasm almost shouted. "And so good to meet you in person." He looked away, out the window, and lowered his voice. "I have to admit I'm nervous to the point of shaking." He smiled as if to reassure himself and turned back to me. Our hands found each other and locked below the sight line of the East Indian driver. "I can't tell you how good it feels to hold your hand," he said. I could feel a slight trembling.

"Yes, it does." I smiled warmly at him, but my critical faculties were active: Despite his pleasant, beaming face and boyish mien, Will was not classically handsome. His teeth had irregularities. He wore thick black eyeglasses—in his photo they made his eyes sag like a beagle's. The fresh-from-the-gym outfit was problematic—his jersey overshirt sported a large embossed star; his trendy three-quarter casual slacks teemed with Velcro. He wore a thick silver chain around his neck and clunky sandals on his feet. But the gestalt somehow appealed to me. It was an evening that would pass pleasantly. And our hands had struck an immediate rapport, fingers folding naturally into each other.

As we inched through the traffic, I pointed out the sights— the theater district, Columbus Circle (his first glimpse of the park), and Lincoln Center. At the Greek restaurant I had picked, we took a table at the window, with a good view of Columbus Avenue.

"Thanks for showing me around."

"My pleasure. Do you know where we are?"

"Generally. It's the Upper West Side, isn't it?"

"Yes. And Columbus Avenue is one of its spines."

"I remember now. I've scoured every website I could find about the city."

We ordered too much, including red wine. Neither of us has ever been able to remember what we talked about that first night, except for a few fragments. We picked at the food, but the conversation was animated.

"So, is the city living up to your expectations?"

"It's fantastic, even just this taste of it."

"After all our emails, I'm still not sure what interested you in coming here. Did you say it was the movie *Hair*?"

"No, that's how I got interested in Central Park. That was later. The reason is so tacky, please don't laugh." I raised my eyebrows in anticipation. "My earliest memories of the city are 'Cagney and Lacey'...on TV? That's when the seed was planted, back in the mid-eighties. I loved that show. Then, as a teenager, I saw *An Affair to Remember*. That clinched it."

"The fateful date at the Empire State Building? What a symbol of romantic destiny."

"Yes," he laughed, "I never thought of that."

"You must be a romantic, Will," I teased.

"You've no idea. I still cry whenever I see the movie. I've got the video, seen it a dozen times."

We discovered we were both avid movie buffs. Will's tastes ran to the big releases—he was impatient for the *Harry Potter* and *Lord of the Rings* epics—and he followed industry news on the Internet.

"How do *your* tastes in film run?" he wanted to know.

"It varies. But I grew up with film noir. That's the way I measure reality. Are you familiar with it?"

"Oh, yes—*The Maltese Falcon,* some of the other classics. I still have a lot of catching up. But they're hard to find in Ireland. The video rental shops shelve only the new films."

"That's too bad. The stores here are a virtual library."

During dinner Will pulled a small gift-wrapped package out of his pack and insisted I open it. It was a book, a recent Gide biography, one my son had also given me for my last birthday. On the inside cover there was an inscription: *A little something so you never forget. Will 2000.* I had mentioned Gide in my correspondence—I was shocked that so few younger gays knew of him. I was touched at his trying to please me. It took me a moment to regain my balance.

"Thank you...you know how important Gide was to gays in my generation?"

"Not really."

"Well, *The Immoralist* was the Rosetta Stone for the closeted. And Gide's diaries were mind-blowing. But I'm waxing on..."

When the time came to leave, most of dinner was still on the table. Will insisted on treating, "I really appreciate your taking the time."

Despite the muggy weather and the threat of rain, we agreed to walk to my apartment. We strolled up West 72nd Street past the Dakota, as I'd planned. Will recognized the entryway where Lennon was killed. As we walked, he lit a cigarette, assuring me he wouldn't smoke in the apartment. On Central Park West, the park stretched out before us. I thought we might enter it—I had planned to dart in and offer Will a first kiss. Our correspondence had nourished that affection; his boyish, warm presence sharpened the impulse. But the park was overrun with people scurrying to a scheduled concert on the Great Lawn.

We reached my building and casually walked past the concierge, who was engrossed in a Latino television show. Once the elevator door shut, Will and I were alone for the first time. From his corner of the elevator, Will smiled at me, a smile that radiated affection and expectation. I recall the moment—it also radiated an inkling of devotion, a spark that emboldened me, freed me to do as I pleased. I moved toward him, pressed him gently to the wall, and kissed him, finally. His lips and tongue were supple and responsive.

"You are cheeky," he joked, when the elevator stopped at my floor.

"We've waited for this moment for six weeks. Hardly a bold move."

Inside the apartment, I took him to the window and showed him the museum view. It had become my standard opening strat-agem. He took it in as I approached him from behind. Before I even touched him, he quickly turned back to me and placed his body firmly against mine, craning his face forward for another kiss. It evolved into a thorough embrace. Our dance proceeded. We poured wine and spoke; our conversation, easy and rambling, alternated with embraces that ratcheted up in intensity. That we already knew each other—the six-week correspondence, the phone conversations—added a familiarity, a sense of closeness, to my attraction.

The signals were clear. While Will washed up, I unfolded and made up the futon. I quickly hid the Gide biography my son had given me, so Will wouldn't notice his was a duplicate. He emerged from the bathroom in snug boxer shorts—he was lovely, a lithe, young male body, a faunlike creature with a light carpeting of auburn hair. He had a gently muscled torso, the

kind I prefer, defined but soft to the touch. He helped me off
with my clothes. When he lowered his shorts I saw he was uncir-
cumcised, his penis large and semihard.

In memory, our first lovemaking was not remarkable. But,
from the start, we shared a sensual vocabulary. Based in affection, it mounted to a crescendo of sensation, stirred by intense
caresses, the wandering of lips and tongues across each other's
bodies, and frequent returns home, face-to-face, for needed
kisses. We coped with the condoms, then each of us focused on
the other's genitals. Once we brought each other to ejaculation,
we lay in each other's arms.

"Do you know how beautiful you are?" he asked. He stroked
my side.

"No. I don't think of myself that way." I recalled the painful
glimpses of my sagging body at moments I came upon myself in
the mirror.

"No, I bet you don't."

"And I'm ancient."

"No, you're just right, more than that. You know I don't
fancy younger men."

"You're the lovely one, Will. But those tattoos on your
arms—how can you do that to yourself?" I noticed he had an
inch-wide Celtic pattern ringing each of his upper arms. They
reminded me of his silver choker.

"Don't you like them? I love them. They're very popular, you
know."

We lay there for a while, our hands exploring each other.
Will seemed exhausted and fell asleep quickly. I realized he must
be jet-lagged. There was no question we would spend the night
together. It was never discussed.

The alarm woke us in the morning. There was no time for
lingering, I had to get to work. Will ran into the kitchen when he
heard the whirr of the coffee grinder. Like me, he was addicted to
coffee, but he was new to the ritual. We had a pleasant breakfast
and cleaned up. Will took in the view in the morning sun. We
showered together and left the apartment at the same time. He
needed careful instructions for the subway back to the hostel,
and then to Times Square, one of his prime destinations. We
made no specific plans, but agreed to stay in touch by phone and
meet in the evening at the apartment. I didn't give him the keys,
nor did he ask for them. It went unsaid that he wasn't to use the
apartment while I was out.

What did I feel that morning as we parted on the subway? I
was exuberant, if a bit tired. It had gone well, without awkward-
ness, hurt, or second thoughts. I had carried it off with my young
friend and that felt good.

By late morning Will called at the office. He had run into two
Irish girls staying at the hostel. They invited him to join them
that evening at a local tavern that featured Irish dancing. He
sounded enthusiastic. I refrained from asking if I could join—I
was aware of the age difference and not about to impose myself.
He would call from the tavern to let me know his plans. Once
I hung up the phone, I realized I had no idea whether I would
ever see Will again.

It was ten-thirty in the evening and I hadn't heard from Will. He
had decided to go on to better things—we had our encounter,
now there were others to be had. The Irish girls were a convenient excuse, maybe a construction. Somber as my disappointment was, I felt a sense of relief. I couldn't deny some lingering
anxiety about having another tryst. At least I wouldn't be
required to perform again. Men of a certain age—many of

them—struggle with uncertainties about sexual performance, even at the crest of excitement. I was no exception. The prospect of failing with a male partner was even more daunting; you could trust women to be more accepting. Another evening with Will might find me—how to put it?—less responsive. If he didn't call, I wouldn't be put to the test.

Suddenly the phone rang. It was Will. "I've been thinking—what on earth am I doing here…with the girls? I really want to be with you, Vic. I'm on my way, sweet—if that's okay with you. It should take me, what, about ten minutes?"

I was stoic. "Stay as long as you like. Just ring up from the lobby whenever you get here."

"No, no, I'm coming right now."

I was pleased. Our quirky relationship was still in play. But I waxed nervous about what to do with him, whether I was up to it. It occurred to me that I should take the initiative. I ought to concentrate on working at him. That might be the best way to distract from any problems I might have.

When Will arrived we had some wine, this time on an already open futon. He was energized about his day in the city. We talked like old friends, long parted, happy to see each other. Again, the conversation became an affectionate seduction—we kissed and caressed as we spoke. He was delighted when I began to undress him.

I held him aside while I arranged several pillows against the wall on the far side of the bed. By now he was naked. He smiled at me—again that radiant trust—while I seated him, his back against the pillows, his legs folded out toward me. He was puzzled, but curious, expectant about what I had in mind.

I took off the rest of my clothes and approached him. Kneeling in the space between his legs, I faced him and moved my body close to his. I started at his lips, with several long, penetrating kisses that he returned in kind. Then, with my tongue, I slowly circumnavigated his face and head, moved on to his cheeks, lapped at his ears, slid across his forehead. Then, the soft tissue above and below his eyes, and every contour of his neck and underjaw. I comprehended each of his features with my tongue and lips, returning frequently to his mouth for lingering kisses. Very soon he purred with pleasure. I was struck by his openness to being loved so.

I moved to his chest, and to each of his nipples, where he was exquisitely sensitive. Then to his underarms, the most erogenous of zones, where the lapping at his armpits unnerved him and his purrs turned to agonized murmurs. His sizeable erection grew firmer. Since he wasn't wearing a condom, I noticed for the first time that erect dicks look alike, circumcised or not. He trembled with pleasure and drew my face to his, kissing me passionately, as if to halt my progress and give his sensations pause. I continued my journey at his arms, and slowly slid my way past the tattoos, along the sinuous contours of his muscles to his hands and fingers, each of which I took into my mouth in turn, and thoroughly bathed.

Then I returned to his lower chest below the pecs. My tongue conscientiously traced the outline of each rib as it arced upward from the central sternum. Will groaned with intense, near unbearable pleasure. At the same time his hands were mobile— he lightly caressed my wandering head, or moved down to cradle and knead my testicles or stroke my cock. It was intoxicating to pleasure Will in this way, and ask for little or nothing back, other than his purring acknowledgment. I was growing confident of my power to excite Will and gaining some confidence in myself. I was eager to move on—his body was a continent I had only just begun to explore...

When I was done, we turned to each other, and kissed deeply.

He heaved a long sigh of satisfaction. I could feel his pulsing erection at my groin.

"No one has ever done that to me before," he whispered. He seemed puzzled at the gap in his experience. As he lay in my arms, smiling at me, he was overcome with sensation, still in an excited state, vibrating with pleasure. I was surprised he could control orgasm for that long.

"I've never done it to anyone before. Someone once did a little of it to me."

"You are so hot…"

"Whatever that means…" Could "hot" correlate with performance anxiety? "Well, it's my gift to you—so you never forget." I lowered my body to go down on him.

"No, now I want to do it to you."

I demurred, "Tomorrow, sweet. It's late."

But he insisted, and I submitted. Will did very well; he had a talent for reciprocity. I responded in kind. The sensations came in waves, from sheer sensate pleasure to intervals beyond any control. Through it I sustained a firm erection. When he was done with me, we were both full of each other and spent with pleasure, yet neither of us had come. To consummate, we applied K-Y jelly, using our hands to masturbate each other as we kissed—we had no use for condoms at this point. Will exploded quickly, in a forceful and abundant stream. I came soon after.

I was so taken by Will, by his young, faunlike beauty, so ecstatic about our physical communion, even more by the affectional bond, that I pressed close to him as we kissed, near to the point of crushing each other. Will pulled his face away for a moment and stroked my chest.

"There's something I've got to tell you, Vic."

"What?"

"I've always wanted someone who comes close and kisses once

we've come, who understands how important that moment is."

"Doesn't everyone?"

"No, most men I've known have their squirt, then say 'Thank you' and turn over."

I was moved. "Not us. No, not us." We pressed together again, kissed tenderly for a while, and fell asleep, our semen-soaked bodies folded together.

That morning I awoke before the alarm. I lay gazing at Will as he slept, his face inches from mine. He was so trusting and innocent. I had not known any man as beautiful, or so well. When it was time, I moved forward and kissed him gently on the lips to wake him. In his sleep, his lips opened and admitted me, responding fully to the thrusts of my tongue, and we embraced closely. In all our years together, I cannot remember Will ever not being ready for, or open to my affection. Or I to his.

LIEBESTOD:
LOVE/DEATH
FINAL ARIA WITH
IMAGINARY MUSIC

Robert M. Dewey

Tom, the old man's lover for forty years, had died. The old
man, having outlived the things of his life, found that he was
now a stranger and alone. Unable to bear so much reality, he
filled his house with memories.

There were baskets of stones Tom and he had collected—
agate, quartz, obsidian, river rocks with mysterious patterns and
shapes, even a bottle of gallstones from his doctor; baskets of
seashells found on beaches; vases of feathers gathered on long
walks—swan, goose, seagull, crow, and the down from some
unknown thing, small and soft; stoppered bottles of dried rose
petals, lavender, mint, and some more exotic, ma-huang, wolfs-
bane, and sleep-inducing valerian root, which the ancient Greeks
called *Phu,* because it stinks. There were books everywhere.
And everywhere else an astonishing incongruity of objects—
bright-colored Tibetan masks, bones, pottery, tiny carved ivory
figures the Japanese call *Netsuke,* weavings they had made
together, the sharp-beaked skull of a starling Tom had spaded

up one fall, a gigantic tortoise shell turned to show its mottled bottom, dried leaves, and gods, so many gods. There was a piano, a penny whistle, many puzzles, a crockery jug holding recorders—altos, sopranos, and a sopranino. Covering the walls, pictures—a framed page of an illuminated manuscript, sketches, paintings, prints.

High on the wall dominating his collections hung a huge painting, in the manner of the nineteenth-century Pre-Raphaelites, depicting an old man sitting in a boat with his fishing line in the placid waters of a lake. He was garbed and hooded in dark medieval robes; a crown sat on the seat next to him. His wounded left thigh bled. On a farther shore a mounted knight holding a golden cup waited for the old king. A brass plaque affixed to the frame read: SIR PERCIVAL BEARING THE HOLY GRAIL TO THE FISHER KING.

Late night in the study, a recording of "Clair de Lune" played softly. "Clair de Lune," the light of the moon rippling over the waters, softly. On a daybed, the old man lay with a black plastic bag enclosing his head, cinched at the neck. He hummed quietly to the music. His hand tapped the rhythm slowly on his chest. Soon he began gasping for air. The tapping hand reached up, loosened the necktie holding the plastic bag, and pulled it off. The old man blinked, sat up, and for a few minutes did nothing but try to catch his breath. Finally he slipped his feet into a pair of slippers and shuffled across the room. Sitting at his desk, he opened his journal. Under the last entry, Number 12, he wrote the time, "*Clair de Lune*," and *gave up at 3 min. 24 sec., not engrossing enough.*

He scanned the cases of CDs and cassettes. Muttering. Muttering. *Here in all this music there must be something so enchanting that I'll stay under too long. Forget to save myself.*

La Mer, *Bruch's* Violin Concerto, La Boheme, *Cher and Nicholas Cage were fabulous in* Moonstruck...*o god, o god, I've got it.* Tristan and Isolde!...*it goes on and on and on. Good old Wagner.* He punched the CD player to the last number on the disk, and Kirsten Flagstad's smoky soprano voice began Isolde's death aria at the end of the opera. *Liebes. Tod.* Love. Death. He sat at his desk humming along, *Duuum Deeee Daaaah Duuuh. Duuum Dee Daaaaah!* Tristan dead, Isolde's voice floats over the oceanic undulations of the orchestra. Endless flowing like the sea. Love. Death. Ocean. Eternity...*This is fabulous. Daaaaam Deeee Daaaah Duuuuuuuh....*

Out of a basket of seashells on the desk, he plucked a piece of dog's jawbone lying incongruously among cowries, scallops, clams. Tom had found that broken jawbone on the beach near Pescadero one summer...*Duuuumh Deeee Daaaah Duuuuuh,* the old man hummed And remembered: *It seemed an eternity we sat on the beach in the shimmering air, drinking daiquiris from a canteen, watching the tide breaking hissing, breaking hissing, breaking hissing against the shore. Tom singing, a cigarette hanging from his mouth, singing. Heigh Ho Kafuzalem, The Harlot of Jeruzalem....da da duh, duh dah da duh, and daughter of the Baaa Baaaaa! God, he could make me laugh.* Out of the old man's memory, out of the undertow of Isolde's aria, a voice reciting something once known: *O lost...ghost, come back again... How does that go? It's got to be Thomas Wolfe.* You Can't Go Home Again? *No,* Look Homeward, Angel. *Where'd I put that?*

He switched off the CD and shuffled to a bookshelf in the next room. He smiled faintly as he read (Tom had put it there) the framed sign tacked to the bookshelf:

THIS SHOP IS HAUNTED BY THE GHOSTS

OF GREAT WRITERS WHO ARE HERE IN HOSTS;
WE SELL NO FAKES OR TRASHES.
LOVERS OF BOOKS ARE WELCOME HERE,
NO CLERK WILL BABBLE IN YOUR EAR,
PLEASE SMOKE BUT DON'T DROP ASHES.
Good old Christopher Morley...*The Haunted Bookshop.*
Tom used to love that book. Absolute drivel. He scanned the
dog-eared paperbacks lining the shelves and found *Look Home-
ward, Angel.* He opened to the epigraph.
Which of us has looked into his father's heart?
Which of us has not remained forever prison-pent?
Which of us is not forever a stranger and alone?
...O lost, and by the wind grieved, ghost, come back again.

He shuffled back to his desk. *O lost, and by the wind grieved,* he
wrote down, *ghost, come back again...*
    The old man reached over and turned Isolde's death aria on
again. *The endless waves of the ocean, endless and unceasing.
Sea Sing. Sea Sing. Un Sea Sing. Love. Death. Eternity. Daaaam
Deeeeee Daaaah Duuuuuh.*
    Tom had such beautiful shoulders. Leather and scented gera-
niums. Through the basket of shells the old man moved his finger
sensuously as if through a pool of water, and the shells clinked
and tinkled like bells. He listened to the shells clinking and
tinkling. Like bells. *Ding-dong. Ding-dong bell. Full fathom five
thy father lies. Those are pearls that were his eyes. Sea nymphs
hourly ring his knell. Ding-dong, Ding-dong, bell. Daaaam
Deeee Daaaaah Duuuuuuuh.* And as he listened, memories
surfaced: *Daddy gave me this conch shell when he came back
from Hawaii. And a bottle of white sand. So many things. I can
remember where each shell in this basket came from. The cowry
with the carvings on it, a gift from Hernan when he came back*

from Bogota. The clamshells from a bouillabaisse at the Gold Coast in San Francisco. The little shell with wormholes, Tom and I found years ago, cruising on the Mississippi River flats. The old man looked around the room. Things. Each one a memory. Ghosts. Ghosts. *These things live only because I remember their lives. I live only because they keep whispering to me. Parasites clinging to each other for life. Drowning...*

The CD of Kirsten Flagstad singing "Liebestod" grew louder. *DAAAH DEEE...God, why doesn't she just kill herself and get it over with? One can hardly breathe in here. Told George to take the storm windows off two weeks ago. Only do gardens. Only do gardens. Damned hothouse. DAAAAAM DEEEEE DAAAAAAH...Why do prima donnas have to go on and on? Get on with it.* The old man reached over his desk and snapped the music off.

Calm down...breathe...breathe deeply, quietly...breathe... breathe. It's near sunrise. I should walk down to the lake...The dawn comes. The dawn comes through the incense-burning mist...and o'er the lake hangs the moon, a white Eucharist... Breathe....

The old man leaned back in his chair and looked up at the painting of the King fishing in the lake, a stained cloth draped over his bloody thigh...*bandage...old wounds never die, they just bleed away...Gone Fishin' Gone Fishin'...only place to ease the pain. Then one day Sir Percival bears to him the Holy Grail—Percival, Parzifal, My Sweet Party Fool Tom (so it declines). One cup of wine, a kiss, and I was healed. Holy holy wholly healed. The land blooms mixing memory and desire. And we lived happily ever after...that was my story...thought that would be my story...and then the son of a bitch died...and left me waiting...waiting...for what? Another Prince? The understudy? Someday my Prince will come again, knock at the door again, put his boots under my bed again. I'll be whole again, whole again, jiggidy jig. Breaking news—Prodigal Son Returns to Diddle Father, Son, and Holy Goat.*

If you're coming, you'd better get your fanny over here—I haven't got all day...I thought you'd be my story...my story... You're so vain...I bet you think this song is about you... The old man sang the phrases over and over again, louder and louder.

When he heard that he was shouting, the old man stopped dead still. *Breathe slowly...breathe deeply...just let things be... no more talk...just breathe. Breathe. Breathe.*

The old man clicked on the CD player and heard the opening bars of Isolde's aria yet again. Third time's a charm. He shuffled over to the daybed. Took up the black plastic bag and the necktie (stupid salmon pink knitted necktie—ugly, ugly—but the knot didn't slip) placed the necktie noose over his head, pulled it wide around his neck. Then, he raised the black plastic bag, pulled it down, tucked the ends under the noose, and cinched it up.

He had always loved taking naps on the daybed. Just a little nap. That's all. *If I can just hold out this time. Breathe. Breathe slowly. Daaam Deeeeee Daaaaah Duuuuh. Duuuum Deeeeee Daaaaaaah. Float on the waves...inexorable tide...washing over, pulling back. Love. Death. The undulating orchestra, the voice floating over the water, yearning, yearning, but never quite attaining, O lost, and by the wind grieved...Wagner. That sly old fox. The yearning is just a musical conjuring trick, sleight of sound. Makes his chords progress toward resolution, but never lets them reach it, instead they turn into another phrase— reaching, almost reaching—over and over always almost there, but never quite, not yet, not yet...Unbearable yearning. Love. Death. Pulls at the viscera...Breaking and hissing....*

When the ocean waves finally reached our feet, Tom put his arm across my chest and dared me to stay...I'll stay as long as you do. And we lay holding each other's hands as the waves rode up our legs higher and higher. When they finally reached my thighs, I jumped up to go, but he grabbed my foot and pulled me down and we rolled on the sand and tumbled in the waves and flailed like schoolboys until I no longer struggled. Then he straddled me and put my arms over my head and held them down and at each wave he kissed me and teased me until all I could want was more. And when the tumbling waves finally reached my waist, we held each other and kissed. And the great mothering ocean rolled over us pouring and hissing, trying to pull us into herself, pouring and hissing, pouring and hissing, and I whispered into his ear, *o god, never let this end....*

THE TERROR OF KNOWING WHAT THIS WORLD IS ABOUT

Thomas Kearnes

There aren't enough words for all the kinds of wanting in the world.

—Richard Lange

P ete was at the age where anything could be turned into a gun. A week ago, he was running through the house, a wrapped piece of beef jerky in his hand, pretending to shoot at aliens. Earlier today, his stepfather, James, bought him an airplane made of balsa wood and Styrofoam. The boy immediately held the plane by one wing and aimed the other at the poor man, chanting a single phrase. *Pow-pow!* It was now past his bedtime on a Saturday, and the boy held Topher at point-blank with a crude instrument made of Tinker Toys.

The boy's mother laughed as she put out her cigarette. "Petey, stop that." Candice grinned at James. then turned to Topher. "I really don't understand it."

Topher laughed and crossed his legs. He looked at Pete, an

amused gleam in his eye, and hoped this masked his stark discomfort with the child. Indeed, all children, once they acquired the ability to speak and ambulate, struck within him a deep unease. Topher paused to admire the grace with which James and Candice had managed to compartmentalize their lives to accommodate her son—well, as it stood now, *their* son.

James sat beside his wife on the lumpy sofa. He bent over the coffee table in concentration, separating stems and seeds from the half-ounce of weed he had bought a couple of hours before, while Candice made dinner. "We try to keep him away from all that shit on TV," he said, glancing at Topher. "You know, all those cartoons now are basically about fucked-up space creatures and freaky-looking animals beating the shit out of each other."

"James," Candice cried and slapped his shoulder, smiling.

"Sorry, but that's what they are."

Pete still stood in front of Topher, his makeshift gun drawn. *Pow-pow!* Suddenly through with his assault, he held the gun in his open palm for Topher to inspect. "See how I made it?" The gun was a construct of thin colored sticks jammed into small solid wooden wheels. Topher remembered the pidgin architectures he had built when he was the boy's age. He always followed the instructions in the booklet that came with the toys.

"Did you build that all by yourself?" He didn't know what else to say. He felt like a domestic failure. He couldn't wait to get high.

Pete nodded and bared his teeth. *Pow-pow!* Topher laughed, but inside his head it sounded hollow, the same nagging falseness he felt whenever another man bought him a drink and initiated a line of questioning that would ultimately reveal the two had nothing in common but that drink.

"Petey, I said stop that," Candice said, her tone serious now.

Pete cocked his head at her and laughed. "I'm not joking around, little man."

James lifted his head from his work and fixed his stepson with a hard gaze. "If you can't stop shooting at Mommy and Daddy's friend, I'll have to take that away from you. Do you want that?"

Pete shook his head, earnestly.

"Now apologize to Toph."

Topher gave the whole room a dismissive wave. "He doesn't have to."

"No," he said, "this is important."

The boy's head bobbed up and down as if his neck were elastic. All the juvenile confidence he had shown as a marksman was gone. "Sorry," he said.

Topher made a gun with his thumb and index finger and fired at Pete. "It's okay."

"Now go to your room and play," James said. Topher looked over at the coffee table and saw that James was rolling a joint. His long, thick fingers twisted the white paper around the pudgy line of weed. James and Candice always made sure to send Pete from the room before they smoked with Topher. He assumed they followed the same protocol when no one was visiting. This realization filled him with a strange sadness.

Pete disappeared from the room, his homemade pistol forgotten in his hand. James and Candice exchanged a brief smile, and Topher in that moment felt the tight bond between them. He imagined himself driving home the next morning to Longview, where he lived alone in an apartment that was at once too large and too small.

"You ready for this?" James asked, handing the completed joint to Topher. He took it and ran it underneath his nose, inhaling deeply.

"We're getting it from a new guy," Candice volunteered.

"What happened to your last one?"

"You know," James said, "sometimes people just stop answering their phone."

"It's such a hassle," Candice added, "finding someone new."

Topher agreed, but not aloud. James never returned the sporadic messages Topher left on his voice mail. His only opportunity to contact his friend came when he saw him online, an infrequent occurrence. Indeed, ever since their first meeting, James's habit of disappearing forced Topher to view the other man's life as a time-lapse photograph: March, they're lovers. May, he's with Bernard. November, an awkward evening filled with James's ebullience and Bernard's hostile stares. April, he's kicked Bernard out of the house. August, he's with Candice. And finally, another November, they're married. That was two years ago, with James springing from the void once every few months, a woeful clown popping out of a colored box.

As Topher took a toke, Candice asked him about school, and if he was seeing anyone. He answered her with small shakes of the head. He liked Candice. She was slim and pretty, her long pale blonde hair forever bunched behind her head with a banana clip. Her cheeks were round, full and slightly flushed as if she had just stepped in from a brisk run in the snow. She often erupted into a torrent of giggles at whatever sight gag or wisecrack came across the television.

"Sweetie," she said, "it's your turn to put the music on."

James took the joint from Topher. He grunted his agreement then took a hit.

"What music?" Topher asked.

Candice smiled and shook her head. "I don't know how it got started," she said. "Actually," she added, punching her husband in the arm, "I know *exactly* how it got started."

"Don't look at me," James said. "You're the one who likes Queen."

"Anyway, Petey must've heard them at some point and decided he just couldn't live without them because now he won't go to sleep unless we put their CD on."

Topher cracked a smile. "You mean Queen?"

She nodded. "All I have is one of their greatest hits CDs, but that's fine with him. I don't think he's all that particular, just as long as it's Freddie Mercury singing him to sleep."

James handed Candice the joint and rose from the couch, saying he'd be right back. She and Topher continued passing the joint back and forth. A cartoon show played on the television, one aimed at adults, where profanity and sex jokes were meant to make up for shoddy animation. She and Topher watched, laughing at every fresh crudity. He enjoyed these nights with James and Candice. There was a blessed calmness that fell over him whenever he entered their home. The house itself wasn't much. There was no central air or heat, dirt clung to the corners and grime etched the grouting of the tiles, and every room featured a slightly musty smell. But Topher felt safe there.

"Did I tell you?" Candice said, blowing out an impressive bank of smoke. "Petey starts kindergarten after this summer."

"Is it already that time?" Topher had honestly lost track. He found it impossible to guess a child's age, even when the child in question was very young. It was a blind spot, perhaps a willful one.

"It's so hard to believe."

"Was he ever in preschool?"

She hooted, almost dropped the joint. "Like we could ever afford that."

Topher smiled and looked away. Sometimes he forgot James and Candice didn't have as much money as his other friends.

They never chided him for his presumptions, which made him regret them all the more.

"It's okay," she continued. "My mom says the main reason you send kids to preschool is for the social aspect, and he gets plenty of that here on the block." James and Candice lived in a row of more than a dozen tiny houses, all in need of paint and insulation. Theirs was the only white family on the block, but Topher studiously never mentioned this. More than once, he had parked across from their house and seen their son sprinting across the yard with two or three dark-skinned boys his age.

"What are you going to do with all that time on your hands?"

"You mean besides work?" she said, and laughed. Topher had done it again, made an assumption about Candice that had no bearing in her reality.

"Yes, besides that."

"I don't really know. Thinking about it, it'll be nice just to have that time with James. You know, we've never really been together for any length of time without Petey underfoot." She smiled at him, as if the notion surprised and delighted her. "Maybe we'll finally get to know each other. You gonna hit that?"

Topher looked down to find he was still pinching the joint she had passed him. He had no idea how long he had been holding it. Suddenly embarrassed, he lifted the joint to his lips and took a huge drag. The coughing fit came almost instantly. He managed, after a few moments, to gather himself.

"You two seem like an old married couple already."

She wrinkled her nose. "It does seem that way, doesn't it?"

"I wish I could've seen it." He passed her the joint.

"Oh, you've seen one wedding, you've seen them all. James looked handsome, I wore white. My mother cried. I think she would've preferred I have Petey *after* the ceremony. Hell, she would've preferred for James to be the actual father. But life just ain't fair that way, is it?"

On a previous visit, James had shown Topher the wedding photos, pointing out with pride that Candice had made her own gown, a simple yet provocative dress that Topher still remembered a year after seeing it. The two men had been alone when James showed him the photos, and Topher wondered—not for the first time—if Candice knew how much James had told him about his marriage.

"Maybe you guys should have a baby," Topher said. Immediately, he regretted this. He felt as if he had been reaching for a tasty snack on a high shelf but had managed only to knock it farther back.

"That's exactly what this world needs," she said. Then, pausing to consider the notion, she held the joint to her lips and let it stay there. "I wonder how differently I'd do things if I had another...?"

As much as he liked Candice, Topher didn't feel comfortable discussing such personal things with her. He felt he was betraying James. He wondered how much she knew about his and James's one-time relationship, or affair, brief as it was.

A slinky bass beat stomped through the room, followed by the familiar, steady rhythm of snapping fingers. This was "Under Pressure." Topher couldn't imagine where Pete might have first heard this song. He couldn't fathom James puttering around the house with this noise blaring over the speakers, and he didn't know Candice well enough to speculate how she spent her time alone. The child's liking of this band was simply a fact of their home, like James's love of cartoons or Candice's laughter.

"You just wait," she said. "When Petey gets old enough, I'm going to play this CD for him and remind him how much he used to love it. I bet he'll tell me he hates it. You know how kids are—show them something they liked growing up, and they'll turn against it on general principle."

Topher smiled. He enjoyed the petty philosophies in which Candice indulged after getting stoned. They were a welcome respite from the heavier musings he and James pursued after smoking pot.

"Have you noticed," she said, "that he remembers you now? Sometimes he'll ask, 'When's Toph coming back? When's Toph coming back?' I never know what to tell him. You just appear, like a leap year."

James sauntered into the living room. He glanced at the television. On the screen, a scrawny cartoon rabbit rotated its large head in a complete orbit, as if shocked by something. "You like this show?" he asked Topher.

"I don't think I've ever seen it."

"No one likes those dopey things but you, honey," Candice said.

With mock anger, James replied, "Woman, what did I tell you about coming between a man and his cartoons?"

As he handed the joint to James, Topher studied his ex-lover. He was tall, almost six and a half feet. He could touch the ceiling without straightening his arm. His limbs were long and thick, coated in a pleasing weight that was not muscle but wasn't really fat, either. He had an impish smile that gave him the look of a sly cat. His eyes were dark and milky. When he spoke, he always sounded as if what had been said before stunned him in some way. His voice was edged with a constant tone of genial confusion.

"I got the munchkin in bed," he said.

"Did you leave the CD on repeat?"

"Nah, I'll just let it play out. He should be conked out before it gets to the end."

"Come sit with me. Topher isn't being very interesting."

"You just gotta give him time," James said and reached out to touch Topher's shoulder. His fingers lingered there just long enough for Topher to become aware of them. "He'll spout off something wise when you least expect it."

After James sat back on the sofa next to Candice, Topher returned his attention to the television. The cartoon rabbit was now running. Running, they always ran in cartoons these days. Topher could imagine the lovely grit in James's voice if he had complained about that. What a lovely sound it would have made.

Topher didn't have to ask if he could spend the night. It had been decided when he took his first sip of beer. On the occasions when he only smoked weed but didn't drink, Topher typically headed back to Longview. But when he had been downing beer as well, he stayed. A long-ago arrest for drunk driving made him cautious. He had told James about this when they were sleeping together. He didn't know if James had told Candice, or how he would feel about it if he had. While Topher watched television, James worked on blowing up an inflatable mattress. With just his lungs for power, he was having a hard time.

"Can't remember the last time I worked this hard for a blow," he said.

"Pervert."

"You know, since you're gonna be the one lying on this, I should make you trade. You know, blow for blow?"

"I think we've exhausted the *blow* jokes by now."

"Probably."

"Can I leave the TV on while I fall asleep?"

"Yeah, Candice is probably already dead to the world, and you know I can't hear shit anyway."

"Have you two thought about having a baby?" The question just popped out, tangible between them.

"That was fucking random," James said.

"I know, I just—"

"We hadn't thought about it, really."

"I'm sorry, I—"

"I mean, think about it, wasn't our getting married surprising enough?"

Topher had to agree. He remembered his shock when he learned that James was even seeing Candice, let alone proposing to her. The two men had run across each other online, and Topher had been heartened to hear that James had ditched Bernard. He agreed to visit. As he pulled up to the curb, he was further encouraged by James's eager wave in response to his own. He bounded from the car, and they sat on the porch, smoking cigarettes, sitting perilously close. Topher brushed his hand against James's thigh, and when James neither indulged nor rejected the advance, he drew back his hand, uncertain how to proceed. James said he had been seeing someone and it looked like they were "going to get together," as Topher indelibly remembered him putting it. When he asked who the guy was, James shrugged and said it wasn't a guy at all, but a woman. A woman named Candice.

"You've always been full of surprises," Topher said as his friend slouched on the floor, the half-inflated air mattress on his lap.

"Never thought my sex life would become so topical, huh?"

"Was it that way when you were having sex with me?" Sometimes Topher took absurd risks like this. For him, it was part of the romantic thrill, the retelling of a conquest to the very man who took part in it.

James smiled slyly, faked a look in the direction of his and

THE TERROR OF KNOWING WHAT THIS WORLD IS ABOUT

Candice's bedroom. He said in a low voice, "You were always a good fuck, boy. You know that."

"It's nice to hear it now and again."

James blew again into the tube, caught his breath. "Toph is a good fuck." He blew again, took another breath. "Toph is an incredible fuck." He blew again, another breath. "Toph made me come twice."

He was touched that James remembered their sex with the same clarity he did. There's no lonelier feeling than recalling an ecstatic memory only to realize no one shares it. He wondered how often James reflected on those few nights they spent in his modest twin bed with the mismatched sheets. Topher studied his ex for a moment, as if he were a deer in the wild he didn't want to spook.

James finally looked up from the air mattress. "What is it?"

"I've always wanted to know something."

"Yes, you turned me straight." He laughed at his own joke. "Seriously, Toph, what is it?"

"Does Candice…?"

"Does Candice what?"

"Does she ever ask about us?"

"What would she ask?"

"You know, how we met. What we were doing…" He didn't want to use the word *fucking*. He preferred to let the image fester in his friend's imagination.

"She's a smart girl. I'm sure she knows we weren't pitching tents."

"But she's never asked?"

"I guess it didn't really matter to her." Topher's hopeful smile faltered as his ex-lover continued. "I mean, she knew whatever happened between us was definitely over, so what was the point, you know?"

"I was just curious."

James blew a healthy breath into the mattress. Its surface rose. "What made you think of that?"

"Eh, just horny tonight."

"That's nothing new. What's really going on?"

"Nothing."

James narrowed his milky dark eyes at Topher, who suspected he knew the effect that look had on men—and women, too, apparently.

"I've been having a bit of a drought lately."

"No nice hard cock for Topher-boy?"

"Nope."

"Well, if this were the seventies, I'd definitely slip you a hard one."

"What does that have to do with anything?"

"You know, the seventies."

Embarrassed, and elated, Topher looked away, his fingers to his lips. "Thanks, buddy."

James let out a gust of air but it wasn't a laugh. He craned his head back over the air mattress. He did not look at Topher again until it was completely inflated.

Topher remembered the tingle he got when James opened the door the night they first met. He filled the door frame from top to bottom. From his picture online, Topher had imagined someone shorter and thicker, certainly older looking. Even at just a shave under thirty, James could pass for someone a half-decade younger. Topher offered his hand, but James simply grabbed him by the shoulder and pulled him in for a bear hug. They remained like that, embracing, for moment after moment, until at last James bowed his head to meet Topher's lips. Topher remembered that kiss with a fervor that sometimes shamed him.

It seemed James was already speaking before their lips parted. "Damn," he said. "Guys almost never look like their pictures." "Impressed?"

"Very." He kissed Topher again.

After that, Topher spoke. "You're hugely tall."

"Don't ask if I ever played basketball."

"I hate that sport."

"*Hate* is a strong word. A dozen grown men in their underwear running back and forth: there's something to be said for that."

"I should re-examine it, then," Topher said.

James picked him up from the floor and looped his arm under his knees. Topher was a slight, slim boy and easy for James to carry. They made their way to the bedroom, laughing as James accidentally knocked Topher's head against the door frame.

Recalling that first time in the dark night, while the air mattress groaned and squeaked beneath him, was foolish, thought Topher. Queen still wailed from Pete's room. James had already left for his bedroom. Topher had glimpsed the room during previous visits, the simple off-white blinds closed over the window, the deep orange bedspread, the shoes dotting the floor. He tried to imagine himself there, waiting for James. What would he say as James undressed and slipped under the covers? How would Topher please him, make sure he fell asleep in total bliss? It had been easy when they were together in bed, a sensuality they had achieved time and time again. He turned over on the mattress, thinking about that wonderful month with James.

Fingertips touched his shoulder. In his half-sleep, he tried to ignore them. He turned his head to find James staring down at him.

James smiled and said, "I knew it. You never go to sleep early."

"Is something wrong?"

"Not really. I just had to ask you something."

Could this be it, the confession Topher had been waiting for? James was in his gray sweatpants and a white T-shirt, his hair already disheveled. Topher was sure he looked awful himself. If this was going to be a conversation he recalled for the rest of his life, he wanted to remember it differently.

"What is it?" he asked.

"You remember what you said about me and Candice having a baby?"

"I think so."

"Well, do you think I'd make a good dad?"

"You're already a dad. What about Petey?"

"It's different when the kid's not yours."

"How so?"

"It's hard to explain without sounding like an asshole."

"You are an asshole."

"Stop being funny," James said. "I'm serious."

"I know."

"So what kind of father would I be?"

"I don't know." Topher propped himself up on an elbow. "That's a weird question."

"You're the one who brought it up."

"I was teasing you."

"But I wanna know."

"How would I know? We're the same age."

"I can't ask anyone else."

Despite himself, Topher thought back to James lying beside him in bed, thought about how he would describe this man to a stranger.

"You'd be gentle, kind." He paused, thinking. "Giving. I think you'd be really generous."

"Okay."

"And you'd make the poor kid go out and play basketball while you sat on the sidelines acting like an asshole."

James laughed. Topher remembered James chuckling as he carried him off to bed all that time ago. He knew no one would be joining him on the mattress tonight.

"I think we might do it."

"Do what?"

"A baby, have a baby."

James had touched Topher's shoulder again before heading back to bed. Without thinking, Topher had reached out to grab his hand. James did not withdraw from his touch. When he was gone, Topher found himself falling, easily and gratefully, into sleep. Queen rumbled on from Pete's room. He wasn't a fan. He only remembered their big hits, and this wasn't one of them. The music muffled them at first, but Topher eventually heard small footsteps tracking toward his head. He rolled over and saw Pete standing there. He was dressed in his pajamas, a menacing Transformer on the chest. He rubbed his half-closed eyes with one of his fists. In the other, he held the gun made of Tinker Toys.

"What are you doing out of bed, buddy?"

"I can't sleep."

"Do you want me to get your mom?"

Pete slowly shook his head, as if the question puzzled him. Topher felt stupid just staring at the boy, but he didn't know what to say. He never knew what to say.

"If your mom catches you out of bed, you'll get in trouble."

Pete offered up the gun. Topher looked at the toy in his hand, unsure what to do. Finally, he asked, "Is that for me?"

Pete nodded. The music from the other room ended. Silence filled the house. Topher was intensely aware of the cool draft through the windows, the old and ugly sofa, how the air mattress squeaked and sighed under his weight. He wanted very much to leave this house, perhaps never come back. But where would he go this late at night? He took the gun from Pete.

"Do you care if I make something else with this?"

Pete shook his head. Topher began dismantling the gun, pulling the colored sticks from the wooden spokes. He worked quickly, surprisingly immersed in the task. "Yeah," he said, "let's make something better with this."

"What are you making?"

"Something else, something that can't hurt anyone. Doesn't that sound nice?"

AFFLICTED

J. M. Snyder

The first time I saw him naked, I noticed the cuts.

Red, angry scrapes across the pouch of his lower belly, like scratches or claw-marks. "What's this?" I asked, running a finger over one bumpy scab.

He sucked in his gut to pull out of reach. "Nothing." His voice turned sullen, pouting, and the erection that jutted from his thick crop of black curls seemed to wilt a little. "I thought we were going to—"

"Did you do this?" I asked, interrupting him. The cuts bothered me; they spoke of a pain I didn't know how to deal with, and that scared me. *He* scared me. I thought I'd known him.

When he didn't reply, I looked up from the cuts and saw the answer in his eyes. Sad, dark eyes, downcast, like the sky before a storm. He couldn't seem to meet my gaze, as if the cuts embarrassed him, or he was ashamed of his own weakness. "Where else do you do this?" I asked.

Still no answer, but his arms moved behind his nude hips as

if hiding from my view, and I snatched his right elbow to see for myself. In the low lamplight of my dorm room, I could see very faint traces across his skin, a network of healed flesh. With a hard tug, I pulled him over to my bedside table and turned the lamp up higher, held his arm beneath it. "Please," he said, trembling when my fingers trailed over the scarred flesh. "It's nothing, okay? Those are so old."

Holding his arm aside, I pointed at his stomach. "These aren't."

His hand covered the fresh marks as if he could smooth them away, but he didn't say anything and I knew I was right. Sinking down to sit on my bed, I guided him into the space between my legs and wrapped my arms around his thighs. Ignoring the hard dick pointing at me, I pressed my face to his belly and kissed the highest cut, just below his navel. His hands cradled my head, fingers delving in my hair, and I waited for him to sigh my name before I admonished, "This doesn't happen again."

No response.

My hands curved around his buttocks, rubbing the firm flesh, my fingertips meeting in the cleft between his cheeks. I kissed the next cut, a little lower, then the next, and the next, until my chin grazed the bushy hair at his crotch. Bending down, I planted my lips on his thick shaft, then paused. His skin quivered beneath my breath, and his hands fisted in my hair. "You hear me?" I asked, looking up the lean length of his body to meet his hooded eyes.

The hands on my head tried to push me down but I refused to budge. "Yes," he sighed. I waited, wanting more. "Yes, please. I promise, all right? I swear, just…"

His words dissolved into a gasp of delight as I took him in my mouth. With my lips, my tongue, my hands, I tried to show him what I felt for him, the love and desire I felt for this body against

mine. I hoped he'd remember that the next time he wanted to
tear into it.

It was the first nice day of spring. Though patches of snow still
clung to the ground, refusing to melt, the sun beat down strong
through the scant breeze, warming the air. I couldn't be bothered to sit in class on a day like that, so we met at the bus stop
on campus with plans to head into DC for the day. When he
approached, my good mood dissolved at the sight of the black,
long-sleeved T-shirt he wore. "Aren't you hot in that?" I asked.

Nudging his hip against mine, a playful gesture that belied
his haunted eyes, he teased, "If you think I am."

When I touched his arm, he pulled away. I wanted to grab
his elbow, slide up his sleeve, and see what he might be trying to
hide. But we weren't alone—other students waited for the bus,
most of them heading into town like us. So I let him distract me
with small talk and that pretty smile of his, those shy eyes, and
waited for my chance.

A half hour later we were at the Metro station, buying
tickets for the train. Before he could head through the turnstile,
I snagged the back of his shirt. "This way," I said, nodding at
the restrooms. When he hesitated, I added, "Come on, man. I
gotta take a leak."

The men's room was empty, a minor miracle. He went right
to the sinks, leaning over one of them to study his reflection in
the mirror as he waited for me. But I didn't stop at the urinals—I
came up behind him, my arms encircling his waist, my whole
body pressed against his back. My head fit neatly between his
shoulder blades. With a laugh, he touched my hands, folded
over his belt. "Right here?" he asked, his voice coy.

Outside the restroom, footsteps rang off the concrete floor,
heading our way. Without releasing him, I backed into the

nearest stall; he laughed again, letting me pull him along. When he latched the stall door, locking us in, I stepped back and picked at the bottom of his shirt. "Take this off."

The stall was cramped. He turned, bumping against me; I caught the hem of his shirt, tugging it up over his flat, hairless stomach. "Wait," he said.

I raised the shirt higher, exposing pert nipples that hardened in the restroom's cool air. "What are you doing?" he asked with a shaky laugh, trying to smooth the shirt down. "Wait…"

I couldn't. Merciless, I pulled the shirt up over his head and he bent at the waist to let me take it off. His black curls were disheveled, his face ruddy, his arms and chest pimpling with goose bumps that he tried to rub away. Tucking one of his shirt-sleeves into my back pocket to keep it from falling to the floor, I caught his wrist and had to fight him to turn his arm over. He struggled, his other hand clawing at mine to keep me from looking, but I was the stronger man.

On the inside of his arm, up near his elbow, were a series of bloody marks.

Anger flared in me at the sight of the swollen, damaged flesh. "You told me you'd stop this."

He twisted out of my grip, all playfulness gone. "You're not the boss of me," he said, sullen. "Give me back my shirt."

Instead I grabbed his arm again, my fingers closing over the recent cuts. He drew in his breath, hissing in pain. "You think this hurts now?" I asked, squeezing harder. He gasped and tried to pull away but I wouldn't let him go. "Why do you do it in the first place?"

"I don't know," he mumbled. "Please—"

"When do you do it?" I wanted to know.

"Please," he sobbed.

Without warning I released him. Before he could draw his

thin arms in across his chest and shut me out, I stepped closer, pressing my body to his. Cradling his head in my hands, I touched my forehead to his and forced him to look at me, to see *me*. I stared into his teary eyes and waited, silent, for the apology I knew would come.

He drew in a ragged breath that hitched in his throat. I felt his hands touch my back, tentative, then fist in my shirt as if clinging to me for support. "I'm sorry," he sighed, face crumpling beneath a pain I didn't understand. "So sorry. I didn't think—"

I kissed his words away. "This hurts me, too," I whispered; he nodded, yes, he knew. "To see you do this, and not even know why. Do you get off on it?"

He shook his head, and my hands tightened on his face as if I could somehow pour my own strength into him.

"Do you like it?" I asked.

Another shake.

A cloying helplessness rose in me, and I clenched my teeth in frustration. "Then why?"

Through his tears, he whispered, "I don't know. I'm sorry."

I kissed him again, a hard, rough kiss that pinned him back against the stall door. I gave him myself in that kiss, everything I had, everything I felt, as if I could somehow hollow out all the pain trapped in him and instead fill him up with something happy, something positive. Fill him up with me.

Wasn't that enough?

We missed our train. Instead, I led him outside, to a grassy hill that overlooked the rails, and we lay together in the thin sunshine, me on my back and him on top of me, once again holding me tight. His head fit comfortably under my chin, and I liked the press of his body against mine. Beneath my hands he felt so frail, birdlike, his shoulders hunched like damaged wings. After a long bout of brooding silence, he whispered into my shirt, "I won't do it again."

"Don't lie to me."

There was no harshness in my words, but he flinched as if I had struck him. I rubbed his back, and beneath my fingers, his T-shirt burned from the sun. The sleeves had been pulled up, but not enough to show his scars. I felt helpless in his arms, knowing that no matter how tightly I held on to him, he'd still manage to hurt himself when I wasn't looking. Why he'd do it was beyond me. How could I ever hope to stop something I didn't understand in the first place?

"Usually it happens at night," he whispered, startling me. His voice was muffled, his face turned against my chest so that his breath tickled under my collar and along my neck. When I didn't respond, he ran a hand along my side, a ticklish touch, and told me, "I don't mean to, I swear. But sometimes, when everyone else is asleep and I'm lying there, wide awake, I can't turn off my mind. I just keep thinking, round and round in circles, until I'm…"

He shrugged, settling closer to me, and I wrapped both arms around his body to hold him. "Until what?"

Burying his head against my chest, he sniffled, upset again. I hugged him tight. If only I could take this pain away. "I don't know," he murmured. My shirt grew damp with his tears. "Until I can't think anymore, and everything in me hurts so *bad*."

"Everything what?" I asked. "What hurts?"

His answer was a shake of his head, rubbing his face against me. "I just need to bleed it out," he sighed. "You know what I mean? If I can just get it out, make it hurt on the outside, maybe then it won't hurt so much inside, see?"

No, I didn't. I couldn't. "What hurts?" I asked again.

"Just..." All the tension went out of him and he lay on me heavier than before, limp now, his entire body molded to mine. He kissed my neck, just under my chin, his mouth ticklish on my Adam's apple. "I don't know," he breathed into my skin. "Maybe my heart."

My own heart squeezed in sympathy at his words.

The ride back to campus was silent. I sat by the window of the bus, staring at the cars passing us, my mind empty because I didn't know what to think about. Him, mostly. At one point, he laced his fingers through mine and held my hand in both of his. When the bus stopped at campus, he told me, "I swear it won't happen again."

"Bullshit." I pulled my hand from his and followed him off the bus. Before he could reach for me, I shoved my hands into the pockets of my jeans.

Undeterred, he looped his arm through mine. "I'm really sorry," he started.

"You want to promise me something?" I asked.

He nodded, eager to please.

I stopped walking, forcing him to stop, as well; he turned toward me, the look in his eyes hopeful, expectant, and not a little bit afraid. In that moment, I knew I loved him.

I said, "Promise me the next time you want to cut yourself, you call me first."

His mouth pursed in thought; his gaze dropped to my chin, then my belt, then my shoes, as if he were too ashamed to look at me straight on. I waited—this was it. If he couldn't promise to at least give me warning that he wanted to hurt himself, if he couldn't help me help him, then I would have to walk away. As much as it would tear my world apart, I would have to call it quits. I wasn't going to fight him just to keep him safe. I couldn't.

"Mostly it's at night," he whispered. I had to lean closer to hear his words, they were so quiet. "Like, really late. You'll be asleep and I wouldn't want to wake you—"

"I want you to." He glanced up at me, hope shimmering in his dark eyes, and I smiled because I thought he needed to see it. "No matter how late it is. Call me, you hear? Before you go too far."

He thought about it a moment, then nodded. "All right. I can do that."

"Cause if you don't?" I added. His gaze flickered to my face again, the fear bright in his eyes. "We're through."

"No." Both of his hands grasped my arm. "I'll call you. I promise."

I leaned in to claim a quick kiss. "I hope so."

The phone rang at quarter after three in the morning. I was still asleep as I stretched an arm out to snag the receiver off my bedside table, but hearing my name in his tearful voice woke me in an instant. I squinted at the digital clock, my whole body numb. "What's wrong?"

"You said to call you," he reminded me. He sounded so small, so distant and lost, a million miles away from the comfort of my warm bed and the fuzzy remnants of sleep that still clung to me. "When I…wanted to—"

Shaking my head to clear it, I said, "Don't do it, you hear me? I'm coming over."

"But—"

I slid out of bed, clicking on the lamp and blinking in the sudden light. "Don't do anything until I get there." He sighed, a lonesome sound that filled my ear. "Promise me. I'll be there in three minutes."

"You don't really have to," he started.

But I was already pulling up my jeans, stepping into my sneakers as I zipped up the pants. "I'm on my way."

His dorm was on the opposite side of campus, but there was no one out that early and I cut through the woods despite the late hour. When I passed the student union building, I broke into a run, sprinting the last few yards to the student apartments. He lived on the second floor; in the predawn silence that draped the campus, my footsteps rang out on the metal stairs like judgment. At his door, I hesitated, unwilling to pound against the wood and wake his roommates, but that wasn't necessary—the knob turned in my hand, unlocked.

Inside, the living room was dark. The only light came from the small bulb above the oven; it spilled across the tiny kitchenette and splashed against the back of the sofa that separated one area from the other. Stepping inside the apartment, I eased the door shut behind me and waited a moment for my eyes to adjust to the scant light. The door to the first bedroom was closed; I crossed the length of the apartment and peered down the dark hall to see the other bedroom door also shut. He slept in that room, I knew, but I didn't want to barge in, not if his roommate were asleep. Would he have called from there?

A shuddery sigh behind me made me turn. He was lying on the floor of the living room, curled into a tight ball as if trying to protect himself from the rest of the world. His arms were clasped tight around legs folded against his chest, his head buried between his knees. Stepping around the sofa, I sank down to the floor, one hand reaching for him. "Hey there," I breathed.

Beneath my hand, his bare arm was cold. His fingers had turned white where they gripped his elbows, as if he held on tighter than was necessary. With a sniffle, he raised his face toward mine and I saw the light from the stove shine in his dark eyes. "I can't," he sighed. "I just can't."

I didn't ask for clarification. There on the coffee table behind me sat an open box of razor blades; I could see from the glimmer of metal inside the box that most of them were gone. Sure enough, a thin blade gleamed farther along the table, its sharp edge flecked with dark blood.

My heart jumped in my chest. Suddenly I was all over him, prying his hands from his elbows, unfurling his arms, stretching out his legs to search for where he might be bleeding. All I found were superficial cuts on his thumb and forefinger, already healing. As I scrutinized them, he explained, "I picked it up out of the box the wrong way. I didn't mean…"

Before he could explain further, I caught him in a tight embrace and pulled his thin body against mine. After a moment's hesitation, his arms encircled me, hugging me with a fierceness I'd never felt in him before. Into my shoulder, he whispered, "Sometimes I think no one cares."

I leaned back so I could look at him. Was he serious? He couldn't seem to meet my gaze. "You had asked why I did it," he said. "Remember?"

With a nod, I encouraged him to continue. He glanced past me at the razor on the table, but I still held him tight, preventing him from reaching for the blade. "Tonight was just bad," he admitted, his voice pouty, sulking, "in so many ways. I was lying in bed and all I could think about was no one gave a shit about me, you know? No one would care if I…I don't know, if I wasn't here anymore, no one would even notice."

Dropping his gaze to my neck, he toyed with the collar of my jacket as if unable to look me in the eye. His chin crumpled and he blinked back tears he refused to give in to. He seemed unable or unwilling to say any more.

I placed a finger under his chin and raised his face until he looked at me. At *me*. When I pressed my mouth to his, I tasted the salt of his tears. "I'd notice." I murmured into him. "Don't I count?"

His answer was in his hungry kiss. I gave myself over to him, hands and lips claiming every inch of his beautiful, damaged body as I struggled to prove to him just how worthy he was of my love.

STARTING OVER

Sam Sommer

You couldn't help but notice the color of the sky," he gushed with a smile big as all outdoors. "It was this simply amazing, deep, vibrant shade of blue; the way you always imagined the sky should be; a true blue, devastatingly rich—cerulean blue, lapis blue, blue velvet."

"You sound like an artist."

"I once was, remember? I had begun to forget that myself." He took a sip from his glass. "Now I completely understand the attraction Georgia O'Keeffe had to America's southwest: the clean, unadorned colors; the clarity of form, the simplicity of line, unending vistas culminating in an explosion of impossible majesty and grandeur—the American Rockies—just amazing."

"And you're a poet now as well, it seems."

"There is poetry there. Indeed there is. And the clouds, Elyse," he went on. "Great lumbering, marshmallow behemoths, snagging tops of mountains as they floated in that ultimate sea of blue, casting their enormous shadows over the land for as far as the eye could see. It was staggering. You had to be there. It's difficult to describe, to do it justice."

"I get the feeling, really I do. You've managed to convey it all quite well, actually." Elyse glanced down at her menu. "I'm sure it's all you say it is, probably more. I'm glad you had a good time. You'll have to show me the pictures one day."

"Is something wrong?"

"No, of course not; why would you say that? But we should order before the waiter forgets about us."

It had been Taylor's first tentative visit to New Mexico, but he already knew he'd be returning very soon. There was something corporal and life affirming about the place, something that whispered to him at night while he drifted off to sleep—a lullaby in tones of copper and turquoise, desert flower and sagebrush, purple and gold, a stark cleanness that appealed to him like age-old, sun-bleached wood or terra-cotta tiles. There was simply a feeling of comfort—of home. Something he'd been searching for without knowing it. Something he hadn't felt since he'd moved out of his parents' house twenty years earlier.

"I saw Michael while you were away," she announced quite casually as she picked at her salad. "He looks well."

Taylor froze in midchew. "Why are you telling me this?"

"Just making conversation."

"No, you're not. You're being provocative. You know I have no desire to hear anything about him. Why are you being so mean?"

"I am not," she insisted, tapping the edge of her plate with her fork for emphasis. "I thought you might be interested."

"Why would I be interested? The man broke my heart and trashed my apartment."

"Sorry I brought it up."

"I don't understand you, Elyse. You're supposed to be my friend."

"I am your friend."

"Then start acting like one."

They sat rigidly, staring at each other, waiting for the other to say something.

"You're being so unfair, Taylor."

"Unfair to whom—you or Michael? Because if you think for one minute that I'd entertain your, or anyone else's, defense of that heartless, irresponsible, unfeeling bastard, you are not only terribly misguided, but completely delusional. I won't hear of it. I won't consider it. And the continuation of our friendship might be in serious doubt. Now, just who am I being unfair to, Elyse?"

"You're not the same person I once knew. I don't know what's happened to you, but I don't like it."

"I'll tell you what's happened to me. Michael happened to me, that's what, and I'll never get over it if I have to hear about him and how sorry he is, or how miserable he is, or how much he misses me, or what a jerk I was, or he was, or that it's time to forgive and forget."

With that he stood up, pulled his wallet out of his back pocket, threw a ten dollar bill on the table, and left the restaurant, nearly knocking down an elderly woman with a cane who was getting up from her seat to use the restroom.

The trip to New Mexico had been an escape: from a stagnant and uninspired career, a diminishing circle of less than steadfast friends, and a lifetime of small yet surprisingly painful disappointments that had all taken their toll. Michael was the last and definitely the most brutal disappointment in a long procession of failures that had Taylor questioning not only his sanity, but also why he continually chose partners who could never live up to his expectations. There seemed to be a pattern. At first they all seemed so sane, so stable, only to emotionally dissemble when things began to get serious. It always struck Taylor as curious that someone who could hold down a good job, be sociable and literate, *and* maintain an apartment in the city and a house in the country, could still be so royally fucked up. New Mexico, it seemed, had cleared his head. It was now obvious that the problem wasn't theirs, but his. He was drawn to emotionally unavailable men like a moth to a flame. No more, he told himself. It was time for a change. A serious, stable relationship might come along one fine day, but for now Taylor would concentrate on the part of himself he was most comfortable with, the part he could always rely on, and the one thing that gave him the most pleasure with the least distress—his sex drive. Taylor was good at sex, perhaps even very good, and he was in the prime of his life. How long would it be before all that changed, before the angle of his erection or the ability to summon it up on demand, as it were, would decline precipitously? Screw relationships! Like Auntie Mame always said, "Life's a banquet, and most poor suckers are starving to death."

The very first thing Taylor did was review his finances. He'd been frugal these past ten years, miserly one might even say. The result being, if he lived modestly, he could move to New Mexico, buy a little place in the desert, paint to his heart's content, and pursue a life of inspired hedonism—hone his crafts, so to speak, while living off of his savings. He would paint and make love, just like Gauguin had done in Tahiti. Live for the moment, he decided. Let the desert be his muse and his dick the divining rod of life. Three years to make it as a painter. Three years to forget about past failures and relationships. Three years to really live for the first time in his life.

The following Monday morning Taylor presented his boss with a letter of resignation.

"It's merely time for a change," he told him. "No hard feelings, nothing personal. I've decided to move to New Mexico to paint and follow my heart, my bliss."

"This is very sudden, isn't it?"

"You could say. Out of character for me, I suppose—spontaneous, and very exciting. I'd like for you to be happy for me."

"You won't reconsider?"

"No way. I'm committed."

"Certifiable, I'd say. Best of luck to you then, Taylor. You're going to need it."

That was that. He left the office feeling lighter than air and more excited than he'd felt in a dog's age. So excited that there was a definite tenting of his pants—the first spontaneous, nonsexual erection he'd had since he was seventeen, when he'd received his driver's license in the mail and taken his first solo trip in his parent's car.

In the next three weeks he sold off a good portion of his earthly possessions, rearranged his finances, and bid a fond farewell to everyone and everything he knew. Heeding Horace Greeley's encouraging declaration of old to "Go west, young man," Taylor was going west. The smell of excitement permeated the air like ozone after a lightning storm.

Taylor rented a car at the airport in Albuquerque and drove to Santa Fe. He checked in at a centrally located motel and immediately sought out the expertise of several gay-friendly real estate agents to help him locate a permanent address. He was in the market for something tucked away from the city, something earthy and inspirational, but mostly, something inexpensive. It took several weeks, but eventually, a small semifurnished, adobe-style house on the outskirts of town that was in need of a modicum of repair and had the look and feel that Taylor had in mind, came on the market. He immediately put down a deposit, located an attorney, and closed on the property the following month. He moved in with two suitcases, a roll of canvas, and several boxes of art supplies, followed by a week's worth of groceries and a used TV that he found at a thrift shop. Things were beginning to fall into place.

Santa Fe wasn't New York, San Francisco, or for that matter, Atlanta. There was no gay neighborhood to speak of, or hard-driving, frenetic nightlife to be found. Action in Santa Fe meant hooking up at a local pub or a gay-owned or gay-patronized establishment, or else turning to the ever present and dependable online connection. Once Taylor got settled in, unpacked, and into a routine of sleeping until noon and painting until dinner, he began scanning the Internet for places to go and, with any luck at all, people to see. It took some getting used to, but once you got the hang of it, Santa Fe was as gay a city as any other—fifteen to twenty percent of the population, if the statistics were to be believed.

His first hookups were uninspiring and he wondered if he'd made a mistake leaving the only place he had ever called home, streets he knew like the back of his hand, the city where sex could be found just about anywhere and at any time of day or night. Was he now going to miss all of that? But as fate would have it, date number four was the charm, and very charming as well. He was handsome, intelligent, gainfully employed, with the welcome distinction of being prodigiously endowed by his creator. In the past, those impressive attributes would have really mattered to Taylor—a prerequisite for a good and stable relationship; but this was the new improved model, the *I don't want or need a relationship, just let me have some really good sex* version. And to Taylor's great pleasure and surprise, Mark was that as well. In fact, he was just about the best sex Taylor had ever had.

There was immediate chemistry the minute Mark walked through Taylor's door, invoking a small, but fervent voice deep inside both of them that silently exclaimed, *Wow!*

Taylor opened a bottle of red wine and offered Mark a glass.

"If you're trying to seduce me it really isn't necessary," Mark said, taking the glass from him.

"No, I simply thought it would be a nice thing to do."

Mark sipped the wine, approved with a nod, and with some residual wine in his mouth, slid over to Taylor's side of the sofa and proceeded to kiss him. It was tremendously erotic. The kissing was soft and tentative at first but quickly became more intense. When Mark began to remove his clothes Taylor abruptly stopped him.

"No, please, let me," he insisted, and began to slowly and deliberately undress him, taking in every curve, every nuance of his body, while he licked and kissed his way down Mark's unpretentiously muscled body.

"You've done this before," Mark teased, lying on his back enjoying the moment.

"Just a few times—practice makes perfect."

When they were both completely naked Taylor suggested that they move into the bedroom where they could be more comfortable.

Standing beside Taylor's bed, they held tightly to each other, kissing as if they couldn't get enough. They finally tumbled onto the bed, Taylor straddling Mark, pinning his arms above his head, and licking the soft, downy hairs of his underarms. This was met on Mark's part by two seemingly inconsistent responses: laughter and genuine pleasure.

"I'm a bit ticklish, but please, don't stop."

When he was unable to take any more, he flipped Taylor over onto his back and proceeded to reciprocate, slowly moving down Taylor's chest and then on to his nipples, which were now standing at attention, begging to be played with. Mark obliged.

"You make me feel like I came with an instruction manual," Taylor voiced rather breathlessly. "You seem to know exactly what I like."

"I believe we're just on the same wavelength—we like the same things."

"Isn't that convenient."

Mark licked and kissed his way down Taylor's torso while lightly running his hands over his thighs and calves. It was stimulating and relaxing at the same time. Even before Mark's lips came in contact with Taylor's cock he had him groaning with anticipation; but Mark wouldn't give him satisfaction, not quite yet. He continued to tease and lick the sensitive area where Taylor's legs and groin met, slowly descending down to his scrotum, which he caressed lovingly with his tongue, eventually rising up the underside of the shaft and devouring the ample and swollen member down to its very base, causing Taylor to instinctively gasp and arch his back as if he'd been given an electrical shock.

"Oh, my god!" Taylor called out. "That's absolutely incredible."

"You ain't seen nothin' yet," Mark replied with an impish grin.

"Perhaps, but if the feature film is nearly as good as the trailer, I'm giving it four stars."

They played like that for almost an hour before moving on to more athletic activities, all the while negotiating each new situation with careful consideration of what the other responded to and enjoyed, their bodies fitting perfectly together as if they'd been molded that way. Every movement, scent, image of the other brought erotic delight. They each knew just how to bring the other to the point of climax without actually getting there, heightening the experience and prolonging the pleasure. And they knew how to kiss—their mouths were meant for love-making. The sex went on until the wee hours of the morning, until they were both drained and near exhaustion.

"Where are you going, Mark? It's late. You're certainly welcome to stay the night."

"I appreciate the offer, honestly, but I can't."

"Why not?" Taylor asked, wondering if he'd done something wrong.

"It's nothing you did," Mark replied, as if he'd read Taylor's mind. "I just make it a habit of never getting too involved. I try and check my heart at the door. It keeps things simple. First I spend the night, then it's breakfast in bed, and before you know it, we're picking out china. I like you, Taylor. I like you a lot, and the sex was indescribable. Let's just leave it that way." He wrote his cell number on a piece of paper by the bed. "You already have my email address. We can do this again in a few weeks if you'd like, but I suppose that's up to you." He kissed Taylor good-bye and strolled out of the room as if the last few hours had never transpired.

Mark's unqualified declaration of independence should have been exactly what Taylor wanted, only at that moment it didn't feel that way.

In the following weeks Taylor connected with a number of nice guys. The sex was often good and definitely enjoyable, but he couldn't get the memory of Mark out of his head. Without meaning to he'd been comparing each one of them to the man who had left him in those early morning hours a few weeks earlier, feeling just a little lost, and yet so utterly complete. Mark, the man who had insisted on checking his heart at the door, had spoiled Taylor for every other gay man he was ever going to meet in Santa Fe—or anywhere else for that matter.

Taylor consoled himself with his art. After all, hadn't he come to New Mexico to paint? No sense falling back into old, bad habits—to want what you couldn't have. With that thought in mind, he put off calling Mark for almost three weeks, three long, torturous weeks. In the end though, the memory of that one amazing evening won out, and Taylor made the phone call he'd been dreading.

"Mark?"

"Yes."

"Hi, it's Taylor. How are you?"

"Taylor? Oh, yes, I remember now. I'm fine, how are you?"

"Good, thank you. Look, I was wondering if you might like to get together again. Maybe this evening, or whenever is convenient for you."

"Sure, Taylor. That sounds good."

"What does?"

"This evening, say about ten?"

"Sure, absolutely, ten is good. You remember how to get here, right?"

"I remember. See you then."

With that, the phone went dead, and all that Taylor could now hear was the deep thumping of his heart as it raced wildly in his chest. He'd said yes, tonight—didn't need to think about it. That was a good sign, right?

The chemistry between them, once again, was amazing. Neither one would deny that. Feeling just a little insecure, Taylor was careful to edit his comments. What he wanted was to tell

Mark every little thing he was thinking, to let him know in no
uncertain terms how he felt, but he absolutely knew that wasn't
a good idea. He needed to keep this unemotional. What Taylor
was feeling was based for the most part on sex. The truth was
that they hardly knew each other. They'd never even shared a
cup of coffee, or talked about their respective lives other than
the basics. They didn't even know each other's last name. This
was about sex, pure and simple. Only Taylor couldn't stop from
asking himself, if the sex was this good, could there possibly
be more? And then there was the more uncomfortable truth:
the fact that it just wasn't in Taylor not to feel, to hope, to let
himself fantasize what might be if things were allowed to progress. He could rationalize from now to kingdom come why he
needed not to get involved, to break free from his neediness—his
overwhelming desire to be in a relationship; why recreational sex
was the way to go; but melting into Mark's body like a sundae
on a summer's day threw all of that right out the window. So
what if it was good sex—great sex—hell, spectacular sex! That
didn't mean there was more to it—something to hang your hat
on—something to build a relationship on. Or did it?

"What's wrong?"

"Nothing's wrong. Why did you ask?"

"Because you suddenly weren't there," Mark said, while he
continued to play with one of Taylor's nipples. "You looked a
thousand miles away."

"Sorry about that. It's nothing really."

"You were thinking about us, right?"

"No."

Mark turned Taylor over on his back and kissed him. "I don't
believe you."

"Okay, I suppose I was. I'm sorry. I know you want this to
be unemotional, but…"

Mark kissed Taylor once again, but this time just to shut him up. "You scare me, Taylor, you really scare me…only in a good way. I'm not sure I'm ready for this, or for you, and I need time to process it. Believe me, I'm no fool. I know what we have here. I'm just not sure where it's going to go, or if I should be going along for the ride. You see, I have a history."

"Is that so? Don't we all?" Taylor propped himself up on one elbow. "We could talk about it, you know—your history and mine."

"Sure, we could do that, just not right now, another time perhaps."

"Did you want to leave?"

"Hell no! What made you think that? We haven't even gotten started."

That was that. There was no more talk. Whether what followed was sex or lovemaking was anyone's guess. Perhaps it was a little bit of both. What did it matter? Whatever it was, it was stellar, remarkable, downright brilliant.

There was music playing in the living room just loud enough for them to hear: an old love song from the late eighties. Taylor felt like they were playing it just for him. What he didn't know at the time was that Mark was listening to the saccharine lyrics and schmaltzy melody as well, and was more or less thinking the same thing.

When they were finished making love, or whatever you wanted to call it, Mark asked if he might take a shower before going home. When he returned to the bedroom Taylor was fast asleep. Being careful not to disturb him, he took a moment to admire Taylor's body before gingerly pulling the sheet and blanket up over him. He was a genuinely handsome man with a really beautiful, masculine body, but Mark had slept with good-looking, well-built men before. Still, there was something about Taylor that was different, something intangible, something that for a brief moment made Mark consider getting back into bed and staying the night. But the impulse, as well as the heat that was building in his loins, was met with the cold reality of what that might mean. He dressed instead and left as quietly as possible.

The next day Taylor waited patiently for Mark to call. Not that he had given him any indication that he would. It was just a hope. After their brief discussion on the subject of "feelings," he had decided the prudent thing to do was to let Mark make the next move. Two weeks passed and still there was no call from him, and the waiting was beginning to take its toll. Unable to concentrate, he stopped painting, and looked for an outlet for his frustration. He immediately began to search the chat rooms for a connection, only to find that his heart wasn't in it. That was what seemed to be the problem—his heart. How could he be feeling so much for someone he hardly knew? Was it simply easier to fall in love with a total stranger you could imbue with a semblance of perfection (as opposed to a real flesh and blood human being with frailties and flaws), or was there something happening here, some sixth sense that told him this was special—something worth pursuing, something real. Whatever it was, Taylor realized he was going to have to make the next move. He finally called, only to get Mark's voice mail. He tried his best to leave a friendly, nonemotional message, but was sure his voice had betrayed him. Another week passed before Mark returned the call, only it wasn't the call Taylor had been waiting for.

"Taylor?"

"Mark. It's nice to hear your voice. I thought you had dropped off the face of the planet or something."

"That's an odd expression."

"Is it? I've never given it much thought. So…how are you?"

"Holding my own."

"It's usually more fun letting someone else hold it," he replied, trying to hide his anxiety under a façade of humor.

"I suppose that's true." The long pause that followed didn't help Taylor's anxiety any. "I think we should talk."

"Oh, okay, go ahead and talk."

"Not now—not on the phone. Can you meet me somewhere this evening?"

"Sure, name the place."

Mark gave him instructions to a local nightspot. "So I'll see you there at nine."

"Sure. Nine it is. Bye."

Taylor looked at his watch. It was just a little after six. Three hours before...before what? Taylor had the definite feeling it was going to be a very, very long three hours. He also had a really bad feeling about the evening—meeting in a public place usually spelled trouble. It was harder to make a scene with people around. Only what scene? It wasn't like they were breaking up, they were never together. If Mark merely didn't want to see Taylor again all he had to do was say so, or just never return his call. He'd simply have to wait to find out, and the waiting was interminable.

Mark was seated at a table at the back of the club. He was sprouting a few days' growth and looked as if he'd been sleeping in his clothing. It wasn't an altogether unattractive look for him. He greeted Taylor with a big smile and a kiss, which wasn't at all what Taylor was expecting; it definitely helped to calm his nerves.

"So, what are we drinking," Taylor asked, taking a seat across the table from Mark.

"A light beer. Can I get you something?"

"A beer is good, or am I going to need something stronger?"

"I don't know."

"Why don't we forget about the beer and just cut to the chase, as they say in the movies."

"Sure. We can do that if you like. The reason it took me so long to call you was that I needed time to think—to decide what it was, if anything, that I was feeling for you."

"And did you come to any conclusions?"

"There are feelings, Taylor, strong feelings. I just don't know what they mean."

"Well, that's honest, I guess."

"It's more than that. You see, when I told you that I try and check my heart at the door when I hook up with someone, it's not because I don't want to feel anything, but because I can't allow myself to."

"What does that mean exactly?" Taylor asked, trying hard not to jump to conclusions.

"I have a partner."

For whatever reason, Taylor had never considered that possibility. "Oh, I see. Not a problem, I get it."

Taylor started to get up from his seat.

"No, you don't see. Please sit down."

"Okay."

"We've been together for nearly ten years. He's the love of my life."

"That's…informative."

"I owe you an explanation."

"You don't owe me anything. We hardly know each other, Mark."

"He's dying, Taylor. He has a degenerative disease that's slowly killing him."

That, Taylor wasn't expecting.

"Mark, I don't know what to say. I'm genuinely sorry."

"He understands why I occasionally need to meet other

people. We don't lie to each other. That's why I can't allow myself to get involved. Why I have to check my heart at the door. Why it has to be just about sex."

"I understand. Really."

"No, you don't. You see, I knew after that first night together that it wasn't going to *just* be about sex with you. Not because of what you might be feeling, but because of what I was beginning to feel. I don't know how long Nate and I have together, the doctors won't be specific, but I do know that at the moment there just isn't enough of me to go around. The last few years have been very difficult, Taylor. I don't have anything left to give. That's why I can't see you again, as much as I'd like to. You have to believe me. It would just be too painful, and I already feel as if I'm being torn apart. I hope you can understand."

"I don't exactly know what to say. Sometimes life really sucks, huh?"

"Yeah, it really does."

Taylor reached out and took one of Mark's hands. "You take care of yourself. I wouldn't want to see anything bad happen to you. Nate is lucky to have you."

"Thank you for understanding."

"Maybe another time then."

"Maybe, if it's in the cards."

Taylor stood up and left Mark holding tightly on to his light beer. He cried all the way home.

The next day he began to paint and didn't stop until near exhaustion. It was better than drugs or alcohol, and far more productive.

Taylor worked through the fall and winter, dedicating himself to his art. There was safety in staying at home, and comfort in what he was accomplishing—the satisfaction that one gets from

creating something of substance, something lasting. In the spring
he began showing his work. He sold a few things, but couldn't
seem to get any of the galleries interested in what he was doing.
They were complimentary enough when pressed, but claimed
that they wouldn't be able to market what they perceived as
"Stylistically, not what our clientele is buying"—code for, take
a hike, we can't sell it. No wonder so many artists have to wait
until after their deaths to become famous, he thought, when
success seemed to be almost solely determined by the almighty
dollar. However, Taylor was dauntless. He'd given himself three
years to make it, and he was not about to give up until his money
ran out.

The following year he finally got a small show along with
two other artists. It was only six pieces, but it was a beginning, a
chance to be seen. He sent out promo cards to everyone he could
think of—anyone who might be able to help his career—and
placed a well-positioned ad of his own in the local gay paper. He
understood that his work was most definitely homoerotic, and
although the gallery wasn't particularly interested in promoting
that aspect of it (they preferred to describe it in their own adver-
tising as "The Male Figure in Motion"), he knew where his most
promising market was.

Opening night was a resounding and unexpected success. Two
of his paintings sold within the first hour, and it quickly became
clear to Taylor that the work was generating substantial buzz.

"There's someone here who's interested in you executing a
commission for him," the gallery owner informed Taylor toward
the end of the evening. "He's in my office right now. Would you
mind seeing him?"

"Absolutely, I'm on my way."

Taylor excused himself and headed down the hall to the
gallery office. Inside, standing with his back to the door, admiring

a painting, was a figure that Taylor had no trouble immediately recognizing. He'd have known it anywhere. Mark turned around and gave Taylor a big smile. He was casually dressed in white linen slacks and a powder-blue polo shirt, and looked downright edible, even more attractive than Taylor remembered.

"Surprised to see me?"

Taylor cleared his throat, trying to find the right words. "Nearly speechless, it seems."

Mark crossed the short distance between the desk and the door and gave Taylor a big hug. "You're looking very well, and your paintings are a knockout—exceptional. You should be very proud."

"Thank you, I am. You're looking quite well yourself. It's really nice to see you again."

"You know, I've never stopped thinking about you, Taylor, not for a minute, and then I saw the announcement of your show in the paper and I knew I had to come."

"Catherine said there was someone in here interested in commissioning my work."

"I guess that someone would be me."

"Is that so?"

"It seems I'm a real fan. However, there is one caveat."

"What's that?"

"I get to choose the model."

"Did you have someone in particular in mind?"

"Actually yes, I did."

"And just who might that be?"

"Who do you think?"

"But I've already painted that particular model over and over again. Haven't you noticed the resemblance in almost every one of the canvases?"

"I thought there was something familiar about them."

Mark placed his hand behind Taylor's neck and gently pulled
him near. He let the feel and scent of him permeate his senses,
filling him with memory. "Nate passed away six months ago,"
he whispered softly into Taylor's ear, letting his head lean just
slightly into Taylor's.

"I'm so very sorry, Mark."

"It's all right. It was his time."

Mark began to weep, ever so softly.

Taylor pulled him into his arms to comfort him.

"I'm sorry. I don't know what came over me. I haven't cried
for Nate since the funeral," he said. "I haven't been able to
feel much either. Seeing your paintings here today brought it
all back, and I suddenly realized how incredibly stupid I was. I
needed you back then, only I didn't know how to find a place
for it—for you."

"I understood, Mark, really I did. I'll admit I was disap-
pointed at first, heartbroken even, but I used it. You became my
muse, my inspiration, and look what you did for me."

Mark pulled away from Taylor so he could look at him. "I'm
glad for you, really glad. You deserve it." He nervously put the
back of his hand up to his mouth and cleared his throat. "Look, I
don't know if it's too late for this—if there's someone in your life
right now, but if you don't already have plans for this evening,
I'd like to take you out and celebrate."

"No."

"No what?" He was searching Taylor's eyes to see what he
meant.

"No, there's no one special in my life right now...and no,
it's most definitely not too late. In fact, I can't think of anyone
I'd rather celebrate with. Yes, I'd like very much to spend this
evening with you...and again tomorrow, and the day after that
if you'll let me."

"You would, would you?"

"Yes. Is that way too presumptuous on my part?"

"A little. But we never did get to spend a night together, so I guess I owe you."

They stood a few feet apart, smiling at each other, their eyes locked in a silent, sensual embrace, like fireworks lighting up the sky.

SAIL AWAY

Tom Cardamone

The old man remembered when the shore was wild. When he was a small child the town had just finished being a collection of shacks afraid to cross the bay. He remembered that his grandfather talked of a time before bridges; no one lived on the keys. Mosquitoes moved in clouds along the beach and rattlesnakes coiled in the brush beneath the palmettos. The first bridge was made of wood. The width of the bridge was only one lane. Cars would have to stop and honk twice before proceeding. Bigger bridges of concrete were built. In his teens he would ride his bike over the bridge to the beach, past the parking lots crammed with new Cadillacs, nautical fins ready to cut the air, tops perpetually down. He pedaled past the crowded strip and two-story hotels toward the wooded area. Here the road turned to shell. He swam, chased black snakes between the Australian pines, and watched in wonder as a shifting rainbow of dragonflies hovered overhead.

The old man remembered coming upon his classmate, Jimmy,

in the dunes. Jimmy had been swimming and stood naked, smiling
in the wind, as his cutoff jean shorts dried stiff in the sun on a
large bend of gray driftwood. The driftwood blackened from
the water it had absorbed from the shorts. The boy was younger
than his classmate and shied away upon seeing his nakedness, so
carefree and deserving that cloudless day, but Jimmy waved him
over and patted the driftwood for the younger boy to sit. They
fell into a natural conversation. The sky was brilliant with dragonflies, each one a shiny gold. As the boys talked Jimmy reclined
and slowly spread his legs and flapped his arms and made an
angel in the sand. He then motioned with his head for the other
youth to join him. The boy blushed deeply and tucked his chin
into his shoulder as Jimmy further motioned that he should
remove his swimming trunks. His classmate lifted himself on
one elbow to watch as he struggled out of his suit, now heavy
and awkward with seawater and pockets full of sand. He was
worried they would be seen. He was scared because the other
boy was bigger than him and would tease him for not having as
much hair between his legs, but Jimmy just dropped back into
the sand and began working on his angel. The boy did the same,
thrilled by the new sensation of hot sand beneath bare buttocks.
Exhilarated, he was immediately erect. His prone penis quivered
and he felt an impending orgasm rise, so he squeezed his eyes
shut and braced himself. A calm hand on his shoulder: Jimmy
whispered, "Not yet," then jumped up and leapt toward the
shore. The boy relaxed and inhaled the salt air. Cattails wavered
in the breeze and dragonflies hovered.

Jimmy returned with his hands cupped before him. He let
ocean water drip between his fingers and splash on the boy's
stomach and bare chest. The boy gasped. He arched his back
in the sand and concentrated on the sensation of cool water
snaking down his ribs, pooling in his belly button. He dug his

heels into the sand, and Jimmy laughed and stroked the younger boy's hair.

"Have you ever touched another guy?" Jimmy asked.

The boy shook his head no and looked up at Jimmy. The older boy settled back into the rising sand of the dunes, closed his eyes, and spread his legs. The boy understood the question was an invitation and rose on his knees and crawled toward him. Jimmy's legs were more muscular, his hair dark where the boy's was frothy and blond. Jimmy sensed his approach and sighed, opening his legs farther to reveal a perfect sac pulled taut by a wide erection. The dark crevice of his plump ass settled over the sand like a pirate's cave promising treasure. The boy approached, wanting to explore this landscape of suntanned flesh, but he did not know where to begin.

"Touch it," Jimmy commanded with his hands behind his head, eyes closed. The boy closed his small fist around the totem of muscle and felt as if he were touching himself but not. And he felt *right*. Desire melted through the fear and his touch became sure, exploratory, exciting for both. Jimmy extended his legs as the young boy developed rhythm and as they sighed in unison overhead a seagull, too, cried and they laughed and slapped and tickled each other and Jimmy chased the boy around the dunes, naked and glorious with sunlight all around. Eventually Jimmy caught the younger boy and pinned him to the sand. Face to face, they bucked and pulled and came in exquisite squirts.

Jimmy ran into the surf to wash off his stomach. He lingered there, the dark shadow of a promise as the sun neared setting. The boy dressed quickly and grabbed Jimmy's small, worn, striped towel; he stuffed it in his backpack and rushed back to his unchained bike.

The old man remembered returning to the dunes as a boy and not finding Jimmy but sometimes older men, secretive in the tall grass, exposing themselves, always delighted that he would approach, proudly displaying his own solid member. They taught him different lessons than Jimmy, and were often but not always more serious and hurried. Others were marvels of new knowledge: sailors, dark men from other countries who whispered hotly in his ear. These men taught him that such meetings were universal; all over the world, wherever the land slipped into water, men found each other at dusk in the surf, in the nearby woods, behind rolling hills of sand. They pulled at each other and made quiet demands, and the boy learned that he was obsequious but just so; he bent and bobbed naturally like a cattail in the wind. When he could, he would leave the beach with the man's handkerchief stiff in his pocket. Occasionally he would be able to claim a shirt. He would breathe its secreted scents in bed at night: sweat, cocoa butter, semen: the salts of the sea.

When he finished high school he went north to pick tobacco. Other boys went to college, some were drafted into the military, but after that initial summer he returned to his hometown. He came back because he desired the beach. But he did not stay long. With his tobacco money he traveled the coast and sampled the dunes. For years he would work a season on the farms and then return to explore the Florida coast. He dove naked for sponges with Greek immigrant boys in Tarpon Springs. Miami was a glorious city of light and breeze. He drifted to Key West and drank his money away and played with other boys in the surf, their backs to Cuba, laughing that if there were a nuclear war they would have the best tans in the world. When he ran out of money, the bar where he spent it all gave him a job and he waited tables and learned the secret language of queens and realized it would never be very useful to him: he didn't go to the

movies. He didn't like opera, preferring music he could twist to
at clambakes. He loved the sun and a good day was one where
he never wore shoes. A shirt was something unbuttoned at night,
loose, slipping off the shoulder as a sailor embraced him while
they were both knee-deep in the midnight surf.

He was working as a fisherman on a trawler off Cape Canav-
eral and witnessed an early morning moon launch. A group of
drunken men beat him up in Daytona. He drifted toward the
Panhandle and danced with beery Air Force officers in Pensacola
who would pull him into hotel rooms and parade their muscles
for him or lie awkwardly on their stomachs and await an assault
he would resignedly deliver, and not one of them kissed him in
the moonlight like Key West boys. Still, he kept what epaulets
and undershirts he could secret away. While working in a rough
bar in Apalachicola, making no money and drinking too much,
he wondered if his life might be too much without direction.

Mornings he would go for walks on St. George Island. St.
George was a magical barrier island where high sugary dunes
erased the road on blustery afternoons. The heavenly whiteness
of the sand blinded first-time visitors. Scrub and sea oats were
sparse, the shifting sand was all. One morning he witnessed a
porpoise turning in the surf, glistening purple in the weak dawn
light. The perfect circle of his being slid from view only to rise
farther down the beach. And then another emerged by its side.
They moved with an easy and aimless joy. A third appeared and
he thought, "And so it goes."

He found himself back in his hometown and was surprised
that his parents were smaller than he remembered, their hair
whiter, the wrinkles on their faces deeper. He washed boats at
the marina and walked the shore. Men still gathered behind the
same dunes, and he went to them regardless of looks or age. He
wanted to roll through the world the way dolphins spin through

the sea and was happy to meet anyone who wanted to play in the sun. There was a sadness to living in his hometown, though. Classmates and the older people who knew him as a boy need-lessly pitied him, judged him, and he always noticed the same thing—they were pale and tired. Beautiful new homes, fast cars, but rote lives. He wanted to roam again but felt a new sense of duty toward his parents and reluctantly stayed.

He met Dag on Lido Key one summer, a massive shadow against a majestic sunset, orange curls and purple curtains that billowed behind black clouds. Dag approached; both of them were standing in the water, older but fit, deep tans painted them still-young. The silver dog tags bouncing off his chest signaled potential danger. He turned to study the sunset as the other man stood beside him. They stood so still tiny fish schooled at their feet. Finally the man said, "It's moments like this, the still-ness, the setting sun. You can really feel the earth under your feet *move*."

With that a wave larger than the previous slapped their thighs. They staggered and laughed and walked back to shore together.

Dag lived on the beach, in a house on stilts, a house big enough for both of them; he let that be known their first night together. And that first night was different. They joined on the bed with the sliding glass doors open, the sound of the sea matching their rhythm. He lapped the sweat off Dag's neck as he thrust above him. He stayed the night. Dag had a sailboat and the next day they sailed on Sarasota Bay.

They lived together from that point on. He worked a simple job in a gift shop near the shore. Dag owned a construction company and regretfully built the mansions that were swal-lowing the southern wilderness of Turtle Beach. Dag helped him bury his parents and sell the small home he had grown up in. Dag taught him to sail. Their travels were always to hotter climes, exotic islands and untamed coasts. They kept each other strong, running on the beach, cooking for each other, driving out to the orange groves to pick their fill, catching fish off the pier.

The old man remembered the beautiful morning they last went sailing. The seas were rough but the wind gave them great speed. With the wind in his face he was thinking back to when they had first met, and then a dark shadow lifted them. Instantly, he knew the angle was too aslant. They would not be able to right themselves. They were going over. He looked for Dag at the tiller and saw that he was lost in thought, looking back toward the shrinking city on the bay. He tried to shout a warning but water filled his mouth and he was over. Plunged into a harsh white swirl, he panicked and lost sense of which way was the surface, which the bottom of the sea. But he kicked and clawed and finally emerged to sputter and gasp and ache for Dag, who was nowhere to be seen in the pitch of the waves. The underside of the boat bobbed benignly, a tatter of sail spread beside it. Distantly, the back and arms of his lover dipped beneath a wave. He swam, and when he reached him rolled him over. His head lolled back, too loose on the strong neck that had always been an anchor of sensibility. The old man recalled the fear and hopelessness and then the struggle to bring the body to the overturned boat; the Coast Guard; the long night in the empty house. He put Dag's ashes in the sea and kept only a cutting of the sail.

Years of wandering followed. He retraced his youthful voyages south and nearly drank himself to death in Key West. One hungover morning he lumbered onto the pier and looked at the ocean, hoping to draw some sense of peace from the expanse of undulating indifference, when he spotted, far away, a pod of dolphins. They broke the surface irregularly, yet he imagined that underwater they spun with the happy homogeny of a Ferris wheel. And he realized Dag would want him to whirl rather than drown.

He spun back to Lido Key and sold their beachfront home. He danced with devil-masked hustlers at Mardi Gras. He shielded his eyes from the sun, prone on the beach of Baja, as he watched determined surfers cut through majestic ocean. Boys who never came ashore, forever bobbing in the surf, awaiting the perfect wave; occasionally he would find one of their socks stuffed in an overturned sneaker and slip it into his pocket. The old man whirled his way through Asia and tucked the last of his money into the white underwear of grinning Thai boys.

Back in Fort Lauderdale, he tended bar and grew old in the sun. He drank more and more and wandered the shore and watched the sun set and sometimes fell asleep on the beach and woke with the rising sun, happy to at first be unsure on which shore or island he had just slept. He would look out at the sea and think of Jimmy, of Dag, the untouchable boys of Baja, the very touchable boys of Phuket and Pattaya, Key West at night, sailors and soldiers, the arc of a rocket reaching out toward the moon. Men and boys rolled through his memory merrily like dolphins in the surf.

Canvassing the beach for driftwood, he pulled sundry boards back to his shabby bungalow and quietly assembled a raft. He sat on the porch and sewed. He stitched together the coveted underwear and patches of T-shirt and scarves and such. He lovingly mended these scraps into a haphazard sail. When he pushed his rickety craft into the water the morning sun was behind him; the colored quilt of the sail lit up like the wings of a dragonfly, ephemeral and fragile above the waves, but soaring nonetheless.

THE BAKER

Neil Plakcy

Monday morning, on my way to the unemployment office on Miami Beach to register, I decided to treat myself to a chocolate croissant from the little French bakery around the corner from my apartment. I was about to start tightening my belt, finances-wise, but I figured I could afford one last small indulgence.

I entered the bakery, my senses immediately assaulted by the smell of fresh bread, the rows of beautifully decorated pastries, and the French reggae music playing softly in the background. The bell over the door tinkled as I entered, but the heavyset French-woman who normally waited on customers didn't appear.

I scanned the bakery case in front of me. What, no chocolate croissants? Oh, man. What a disappointment.

Then the baker himself appeared from the kitchen, carrying a tray of mixed breakfast pastries, including the *pain au chocolat* I was jonesing for. "Sorry," he said. "My clerk, she has left me. I am all alone here."

He was about my age, late twenties, and about my height as well, just over six feet. But there the similarities stopped. He was broad-shouldered and beefy, with big hands and a broad smile. He wore a white chef's coat with the collar turned down, already spotted with what looked like raspberry jelly, and a white toque.

"Are you hiring?" I asked. "I haven't worked a register in a couple of years, but I spent four years while I was in college working at fast-food places."

He quizzed me for a few minutes about my skills, and then said, "You are a gift from God. How soon can you start?"

"Now?"

I stepped behind the counter and he grabbed me in a big bear hug, kissing me on each cheek. My body tingled, and my cock stiffened almost immediately. Embarrassed, I backed away, as the bell over the door rang and a customer entered.

My shift was seven to three. The other clerk, who came in at one, spent her first two hours in the tiny office next to the kitchen, ordering supplies and paying bills. By the time she relieved me, my feet hurt, my shoulders ached, and I wanted to luxuriate in a hot bath for hours. But it all went away when the baker, whose name was Jean-Pierre, hugged me again and kissed both my cheeks.

"How can I thank you," he said, his French accent making each word as sexy as a proposition. "I know! I will cook for you. Dinner, tomorrow night."

"Okay," I said, as he released me. My dick had popped back up and I tried to turn away as fast as possible so he wouldn't notice.

Back home, naked in a tub of hot, lavender-scented bubbles, I had only to remember the baker's embrace and I was instantly hard again. I closed my eyes and jerked myself to orgasm, remembering the scent of flour and lemon that surrounded him, the touch of his lips against my cheek. In my head I heard him murmuring soft French words as my body shook and milky white cum spurted out of my dick.

The next morning I wore sneakers with thick white socks to cushion my feet. Jean-Pierre unlocked the door for me, greeting me once again with a big bear hug and a kiss on both cheeks. I felt my whole body glowing with his touch—and the memory of my bathtub adventure the afternoon before.

We chatted off and on as he baked. He was excited about the meal he was preparing for me that evening, and he kept popping out of the kitchen to ask if I liked oysters, spinach, chicken, mushrooms, garlic. With each new ingredient, with each time I saw his shining eyes and the sexy triangle of flesh where his collar folded over, I came closer to orgasm.

He lived in an apartment above the bakery, he said. Very convenient when it was time to start baking, at four in the morning. No commute.

I left at three, promising to return that evening at seven. I lounged in another hot, lavender-scented bath, but this time I wouldn't touch myself at all. I didn't think Jean-Pierre was gay, and didn't expect anything to happen—but I wanted to leave myself in a heightened state of expectation anyway.

After my bath, I stood in front of the mirror examining myself. I hadn't had a serious boyfriend for a year or more; I'd worked too hard at my last job, and all I had the energy for was the occasional bar pickup. But I'd kept going to the gym, and my body was toned and sexy: muscular calves and thighs, slim waist, seven-inch cock nestled in a patch of wiry, black pubic hair, six-pack abs, nicely defined pecs and biceps. If nothing happened with Jean-Pierre, I might head over to one of the gay bars on Lincoln Road and see if any of the available hunks floated my boat.

I pulled on a pair of Ginch Gonch briefs decorated with fruits and vegetables, a form-fitting black T-shirt, and a pair of khaki pants that accentuated my butt. Promptly at seven, I was ringing the bell at the back of the bakery.

Jean-Pierre was delighted to see me. He engulfed me in another of his big bear hugs. He took my face in both hands, kissing me on each cheek, and then, unexpectedly, on the mouth. Though the kiss was brief, his full, moist lips sent a jolt of electricity through me. Then he turned and bounded up the stairs to his second-floor apartment, leaving me to wonder if his ebullience was simply French, or something more.

I also got a great view of his ass as I followed him up the stairs. Without the white chef's coat to cover it, I saw two round globes gripped by a pair of form-fitting jeans. I liked what I saw.

"You must sit here," Jean-Pierre said, when I entered his apartment. He stood by an oak table, pointing at an armchair covered in a colorful Provencal fabric. "You like white wine, yes?"

I said yes, and he filled a stemmed glass for me. "Appetizers in one minute, please," he said, and disappeared into the kitchen.

I looked around. The impression was of a French country farmhouse: an oak armoire opposite a black metal baker's rack; curtains and cushions in the same blue, white, and green floral fabric as my chair. The air smelled wonderful: roast chicken, lemon, and a host of other fragrant aromas. Jean-Pierre reappeared, carrying a tray of oysters Rockefeller, which he placed before me with a small bow.

"Smells heavenly," I said, as he sat down opposite me.

He wore a blue-and-white-striped shirt, the kind French sailors wear, short-sleeved and open at the neck. I eyed his muscular arms and large hands as he dished out the oysters. But when I tasted the first one, I forgot everything but their orgasmic taste. "Mmm," I said, and sighed happily.

They were silky smooth, accentuated by the spinach and the seasonings. I'd never tasted anything so good. "You like?" Jean-Pierre said.

"I like," I said.

We chatted as we ate, moving from the oysters to a roast chicken accompanied by a dish of creamy scalloped potatoes and a tray of warm asparagus dusted with olive oil and sea salt. I didn't think I'd ever eaten such a delicious meal, but Jean-Pierre dismissed my compliments. "Is a simple meal," he said. "Because I must bake all day. When I have the day off, then you will see, I make something good."

"I can't imagine anything better," I said, and when Jean-Pierre caught my eye and smiled a shiver ran through my body and my dick jumped to attention. Damn, I thought, this guy was a flirt. But again, I wasn't sure if it was his native Gallic charm or something more.

When he cleared the dishes, I said, "I can only imagine what kind of pastry you've made for dessert."

"No pastry," he said. "I cannot bake one more thing when I come home. For you, I have the chocolate mousse."

I sighed once again with pleasure. How could he have known that I considered chocolate mousse the perfect dessert? And Jean-Pierre's did not disappoint. He brought out two elegant parfait glasses, each filled with mousse and topped with home-made whipped cream.

From the first bite, I was hooked. The texture was thick and silky, rolling across my tongue, and there were hints of vanilla and another fragrance I couldn't identify. "Is my secret," he said. He smiled. "But I tell you. Essence of violets. Just a drop, but the perfume..." He ended the sentence by bringing his fingers to his lips and kissing them.

I remembered the touch of those lips against my cheek, and against my own lips, and I experienced another of those electric jolts. I couldn't spend another minute in suspense; I had to know if Jean-Pierre was anything more than a flirt. I leaned back in my chair and stretched my legs, and with just the slightest pressure, my foot grazed his leg, and I smiled.

Jean-Pierre smiled back and I saw his shoulders relax. "You would like to move to the sofa?" he asked. "I make cappuccino?"

"Yes to the sofa," I said, standing, and making no effort to hide my boner. "The cappuccino, maybe later."

I sat on the sofa and looked at him. He sat next to me, and I snaked my right hand behind his head and pulled him close. Our lips met, and I tasted the chocolate, vanilla, and violets on his. Our tongues dueled together, and my dick throbbed. I wanted to eat him up, my second dessert.

He pulled me around so that I straddled him, my legs wrapped around his torso, our dicks pulsing against each other through the fabric of our pants. He gripped me in one of his bear hugs, and I luxuriated in the feel of his strong arms wrapped around me, his chest against mine, our bodies merging into one incredibly sexy organism.

I reached my hand under his blue-and-white-striped shirt and started caressing him gently, as he nibbled on my ear and whispered those same French words I'd imagined him saying the day before. "*Quel beau,*" he said. "*Quel homme.*"

I thought he was handsome, too, and certainly a hell of a man. I kissed his neck, and he ran his hands under my T-shirt, up my back, and then down under the waistband of my khakis. I don't know how long we sat, making out. The rest of the world disappeared. I was just a mass of sensations.

"Come with me," he said finally, picking me up as easily as he hefted a tray of bread loaves in the bakery. Damn, I love a man who can do that! He carried me into his bedroom, a big oak bed with a spread in another bright Provencal pattern, and he settled me onto it with great delicacy. Then he lay down next to me and we curled together, fully clothed, kissing and fondling each other.

His shirt and my tee came off, and he ran his slightly rough hands over my chest as gently as a butterfly's wing, each touch sending another electric jolt directly to my cock. I thought I might explode.

Then I was unzipping his jeans. His cock was fat and stiff, and I leaned down to take him in my mouth. He stroked my hair as I sucked, and then pulled me off to kiss him again. I couldn't bear the sensation of my cock remaining trapped for a moment longer, so I scooted out of my jeans. I was about to pull off my briefs when Jean-Pierre gripped my hands.

"Good enough to eat," he said, pointing at the fruits and vegetables.

"You have no idea," I said, kissing him again.

He reached over to the table by the bed and fumbled in the drawer, pulling out a condom, which he unwrapped and slid onto his dick. I found a bottle of lube there and squirted some onto his stiff dick, massaging it, then took a dollop on my index finger and began to grease the way for him.

"I will do that," he said, and as he kissed me again, his lubed finger found my asshole and began to work it. I was panting with longing by the time he lifted me up and, with a little guidance from me, slid himself into me.

All that work on my thighs and calves at the gym paid off. I leveraged myself up and down on his stiff dick, as he lubed his hand and began jerking me off. I couldn't hold out for long, and neither could he. I began panting and whimpering just as I saw his body stiffen, and we ejaculated at nearly the same time, him first, and then me just a few seconds later.

I collapsed onto his nearly hairless but very muscular chest, kissing his neck; he nestled his head against mine. At some point we separated, and then I fell into a deep, dreamless sleep, my body totally satiated.

It was close to six A.M. when I woke, alone in Jean-Pierre's big bed. For a moment or two I was disoriented, trying to figure out exactly where I was. Then I looked at his bedside table and saw a note that read *Come downstairs for breakfast,* and I remembered all that had happened the night before.

I rescued my clothes from the floor and shrugged into them, then climbed down the stairs, stepping out into the South Florida dawn for a moment as I moved from the door to his apartment to the door to the bakery. The back door led directly into the kitchen, and I saw Jean-Pierre bent over a tray of croissants, sliding them into one of his big ovens.

My body sighed with the joy of seeing him. He looked up at the sound of the door; his smile was as broad as the ocean. In a moment we were locked in an embrace, kissing and hugging as if it had been years since we'd seen each other, instead of just minutes.

"*Pain au chocolat* for you," he said, finally pulling back. "And the cappuccino I promised you last night."

We ate together, sitting at a small table in the kitchen. I'd never been one for morning-afters, preferring to get out while the sexual glow was still hot, but I couldn't imagine getting up from that table and walking away from Jean-Pierre. In the space of forty-eight hours he had become as essential to me as breathing.

At seven o'clock I moved to the front of the bakery and opened for business. When I was ready to leave at three, Jean-Pierre said, "You will come for dinner again tonight?"

"Are you kidding? You won't be able to get rid of me."

A month later I gave up my apartment, and moved in with Jean-Pierre above the bakery. If you visit South Beach, you are welcome to come by and sample the wares—but the baker is all mine.

THE FOREST OF SUICIDES

Andrew Warburton

For Shaun

I

I slip a Xanax on my tongue and stare out the window at the white sky, at the sunlight that bathes the silvery wing, and for a moment I forget about the men with knives, about the crisp white cotton of their short-sleeved shirts, darkened by the hostess's flowing blood. I don't want to see the redness in their eyes. Or hear the fury in their speech. I focus instead on the woman in front of me, the fibers rising from her folded shawl, the metallic blondeness of her hair-sprayed curls.

II

I used that color for painting when I lived in the "glass-house." We called it that because the windows in the communal room were similar to the "tomato house" Simon kept in Greenwich Village before he moved back to L.A. As long as it was therapeutic, we could paint what we liked. I painted apple trees that represented "growth" and redbrick buildings that reminded me of Boston. I dripped yellow paint over a blue page and called it *Fear of Change*. They loved me for that.

Simon kept visiting me in the glass-house even after his time there was up. Our friendship was said to be *affirming*.

III

He is out there in a loose salmon shirt, smelling of soap and smiling broadly. This evening, I think, he will play the piano in the local gay bar. It isn't advised, not with his history of drinking, but he likes the stale smells and the flushed faces of the men who put their arms around him. Now he stands at the open door, looking up at the palms that spike the pale sky, thinking of just how soon he will see me. He sits down at the kitchen table, looks out through the window at the shrubs in their plots, the borders running wild with grass. In the shade, the oranges are rotting, and over by the wall, the tomato plants are bare. He picks up a magazine and flicks through the thick black pages, runs a fingernail down one smooth page.

There, beneath his gaze, is a nude, male art shot. He turns the page. There, a poem—his name is at the top.

He wants to show it to me—but I'm packing my suitcase in Boston.

IV

The skyscrapers rise to meet us as we edge down over the city. The sky tilts as the plane turns and I hold tight to the armrest. Not because I'm scared. It's like the difference between blue and green. Blue is safe, absorbing. But add yellow and you get green. Green is sickly, like the plane when it turns, or the skyscrapers' closeness. It isn't *bad*. Yellow *can* be bad. But not today. Today,

I'm prepared for anything. Simon is down there, warm and waiting—I can even feel him if I shut my eyes.

V

My first night in the glass-house they put me in a room at the end of the hall. An attendant carried my suitcase as I dragged my feet along the parquet floor. I waited till the door was shut then peeled off my clothes and pulled the bedsheets around me. I dreamt that night that the room was full of lilies, a jungle on every flat surface. The sickly sweet pollen fell dustlike on the tables and chairs.

I woke in a sweat.

Someone was knocking on the door. "Breakfast in half an hour!"

I met him on the stairs. His cheeks looked wet.

"Are you okay?" I said.

He managed a smile. "Yes. I had a one to one, that's all."

"Oh, right."

The look on my face must have suggested fear, because he gave me an encouraging look. "You'll get used to it," he said.

I shuffled off down the hall.

"My name's Simon, by the way," he called.

For a while after that, I saw him only in passing.

Then one day he came into my room uninvited, sat down on the edge of my bed, and exclaimed: "You didn't tell me you majored in English at NYU! I was at NYU!"

I wondered when he'd expected me to volunteer this information. In truth, my parents had sent me to school in New York because they wanted me out of Boston. I can't say I didn't miss home, but I definitely didn't miss *them*.

The real reason for Simon's visit was to show me his poems. He'd wanted to share them with someone ever since he'd been put inside the glass-house, and now that he'd discovered another English major, there was no way he was going to miss this opportunity. I couldn't help groaning inside. My experience on campus had led me to believe that every young, gay, literature student inhabited a Forest of Suicides, always speaking about pain that was best left unspeakable. I thought of the gloomy figures in black polo-necks hugging mountains of books to their chests under Washington Square Arch. But he didn't seem like that at all. His face was soft, the features fine-boned, and strands of fair hair kept escaping from behind his ears to float wispily in the air. His teeth stuck out over his bottom lip in a horsey way.

His eyes widened, staring straight at me, "So, you'll read them—my poems?"

I had to look away as the sun filtered through a gap in the curtains.

"You can't keep eye contact, can you? You know what that means? You're ashamed. You won't let your guard down."

"You're brainwashed," I said.

He grinned, then hesitated, "That language is all I know, since…well, you know."

I did know.

I thought of those dark, empty streets, my feet slapping the tarmac, still warm from the sun and the drum of car wheels. Chemicals coursed through my blood. I ripped at my shirt and the buttons exploded. Car doors slammed. Blue and red lights flashed—and then someone wrapped a blanket around me. I never wanted to go back—

He was watching me intently. I'd been tugging the hairs on my calf.

"Of course I'll look at your poems."

He tapped me on the knee, smiled, and got up off the bed.
He walked over to the curtains. "Why don't you let some light
in here? It's so dark."

"I like it dark."

"So you can sit and feel sorry for yourself?"

"They've got you trained, haven't they? It must be your job
to get the new ones well...."

He turned to face me, one hand on the curtain about to draw
it back, the other on his hip. He faded into the shadows at the
end of the room. The dark suited him. "I was being friendly. I'll
come back another time."

The door opened and he was gone.

Simon speaks excitedly. He plays with his foot. Wriggling it.
Tugging it.

I listen at the end of the bed.

He always felt wrong, he says. He carried inadequacy everywhere he went. Sometimes it went away for weeks, even months,
and he thought, "Oh, life isn't so bad!" But it always came back
stronger.

No one has ever spoken to me like this before. It's as if all this
time only I was real. But other people have feelings, too.

His eyes fix on me, "What about you?"

I jump off the bed and wrap my arms around my chest.
"Jesus, it's cold in here! Don't you think?"

He looks down at the quilt, his fingers pulling at stray threads.
"Well?"

"Well what?"

"I asked you about *you*."

"Look, you can see my ribs!" I pull at my shirt.

He grins. "Seriously, I want to know."

I sigh. My hands fall to my sides. "My story's no different than any other."

"Of course it's different, you dork. It's *yours*."

My "breakdown" is best described using the rather Blake-like metaphor of a garden. *I got bored of watering the earth. I let the stalks shrivel and the lawn yellow beneath sooty footprints. The shed was charred by the naked sun and the ivy drooped, offending the neighbors; I had let it grow across the whole façade. One morning I woke and the horizon was red. It was as if I had bled myself to death.*

He says I'm being evasive. He doesn't like my metaphors.

I turn the conversation back to him.

His experience was similar to mine, but he hurt himself more than I did. Scars decorated his pale chest, dotted either side with stitch marks. He'd lift a shred of skin to reveal the pink-white tissue, and one by one he'd peel what resembled tightly packed petals.

I asked him why he did it.

"There's a trace of something inside me," he said. "A scar on my spine. Some kind of fossil."

"But where did it come from—this trace?"

He paused. "My mother put it there."

"And where is she now?"

"She lives on a yacht in the Greek Islands."

I remembered the picture postcards pinned to his bedroom wall—all pale sand and sapphire water. A photo of a woman in a sun-hat, sitting cross-legged on the deck of a boat—cocktail glass in hand, a Jackie Collins novel in her lap—and a pack of Marlboro Reds on the floor by her chair. A cliché, but it was true.

Simon didn't seem to miss her.

But then Simon was sedated.

VI

That was how I found Simon. And this is how I lost him:
The air hostess smiles. Cracks appear in her perfectly made-up face. I walk unsteadily across the cabin floor, take my place by the window and strap myself in. My hand luggage consists of a well-thumbed copy of Hamlet.

Now everything is either inside or outside the plane. I've thought about this quite seriously ever since we strayed so close to the city. I'm safe, protected by an aluminum wall—but death is only postponed. The outside might crush me, or burn me, or fling me to the ground, but at least I'd be out of here.

VII

My heart thumps. My hands are clammy. The men are standing at the front of the plane, the air hostess's body lying at their feet. I can see the blood seeping through her top. The people around me are sobbing, moaning.

I think about Simon in his kitchen in L.A. I think about the poem he's had published. I know his stories have appeared in magazines and anthologies, but I'm sure he's never had a poem published before.

He stands up. I wonder if he can feel my thoughts. He glances around. Does he know they're about him? He whistles softly. Insects buzz around his face. He waves his hand, presses his lips together—afraid a bug will fly in his mouth.

He imagines a scale, one side piled with books and journals in which his words appear, and on the other, a crisp white sheet with a poem printed on it. The amount of words is so small, and yet it outweighs all the material on the other side.

He breathes in the late summer heat. He can't wait for me to arrive. We'll drive up to the Griffith Observatory and look out over the Hollywood hills.

VIII

The engine shifts. It grinds. Screams follow a swift descent. However long I shut my eyes, I cannot feel his lips. Just the seat vibrating—the press of the woman next to me, suddenly in the grip of hysteria. He said he would find me and take care of me if I ever went through hell again. I promised him the same. But I am on the inside and he is out there. He stands at the table, making herbal tea, the teabag full of multicolored flecks. He stirs the spoon. A sweet, raspberry-scented steam rises from the mug. His chest flutters inside—

He remembers the lawn outside the glass-house where we held a kind of miniature Woodstock. Everyone who sang or played guitar took turns under the arbor. It was encouraged by the counselors.

He points his foot through the grass and listens politely to a man singing a song we can all relate to: "Glory, Glory Psycho-therapy!" set to the "Battle Hymn of the Republic." I watch him watching the singer, his hand flat on the lawn, his body twisting as he angles his shoulders. I'm itchy. I gesture. His eyes twinkle.

We run around the side of the house and hide behind the conifers. Up close, the branches are black. There are spiderwebs between the pines.

I push him back.

"Prickly," he murmurs.

Our lips touch.

I'm worried about my breath. I haven't eaten all day. He clenches the back of my neck, arches his back, and pulls me closer. My chest crushes him against the trees. I slip my hands around his sides and grip his firm buttocks. He leans into me. His mouth is hot.

What is the glass-house for, if not this? This is alcohol. Drugs. This is everything—and when it's over, we can share a bottle of

wine. Just me and him. I know he wants it. It would be so good—
    Before I know it, he kicks off his sandals, lifts his T-shirt
above his head and throws it on the ground. I place my hands
on his bony chest. His fingers scrabble at my belt.
    Smells surrounded us that day. Strawberry. Cut grass. Wood-
shavings. Our sweat—
    They are outside concepts now. Here there's only fear.

IX
What would I say if I called him, as the others are calling theirs?
Would I tell him how much I loved him? How special he is?
How glad I am we stayed clean and sober?
    I imagine it would go like this:
    "Simon." A masterful vibrato, followed by silence.
    The rustle of sheets.
    "Simon?"
    I can hear the saliva moving around his mouth. His lips
smack.
    "Aren't you on the plane?" he groans. "It's six o' clock…"
    "Simon, something's happening."
    There's a long pause.
    "What do you mean?"
    I hear him switch the bedside lamp on. I can imagine him
under the comforter. One hand pressed against his forehead. His
lips pressed to the mouthpiece.
    How strange, I think, *my voice can escape these walls…but
I cannot.*
    Before the skin splits, sucking the inside out, I catch a glimpse
of shining panes. A thousand skies are reflected in the glass—a
thousand suns over New York City.
    I press my head against the rest, take a deep breath and wait—

Simon wakes from a dream of screaming trees. *A jaundiced moon. Snatches of purple sky. The tree bleeds when he scratches the bark.*

He rolls out of bed and slips his dressing gown around his shoulders. In the kitchen, he pours a glass of milk. Takes it into the living room and switches on the TV.

A building is on fire in Manhattan. A huge blue cigarette, smoking at one end. He doesn't look at it properly. He still has sleep in his eyes. He sits on the couch and stretches his legs. The curtains mottle the daylight on the floor. He switches the TV off. Puts the glass to his lips. Wriggles down between the cushions.

The poem starts in his chest. Rises up into his throat and fills his head. Flows down his arms—into his fingers. Nietzsche calls it a *musical mood.* A vibration or a gnat-swarm is how it feels. It has something to do with the screaming trees. *This simply isn't real.*

ABOUT THE AUTHORS

VIC BACH emerged as a gay and as a gay writer only recently, when he reached his sixties and resolved to get close to another man for once in his life. *Kindred Souls* is excerpted from an unpublished memoir—*An Unlikely Pair*—chronicling his binational relationship with a younger Irish man. The author lives in New York City, on the Upper West Side, and has several short stories and a novella in the works. Reach him at vixx@rcn.com.

TOM CARDAMONE is the author of the erotic fantasy novel, *The Werewolves of Central Park*. His short stories have appeared in several anthologies and publications. "Sail Away" was inspired in part by the novel *Joseph and the Old Man*, by Christopher Davis. You can read more of Tom's work at his website, www.pumpkinteeth.net.

ROBERT M. DEWEY says: *"Liebestod: Love/Death" is my first published story—though I am in some ways an old hand at* *the storyteller's art. In my twenties I was an actor, professional theater director, and theater arts instructor. I received a master's degree in theater arts from the University of Washington and completed all but my dissertation in the theater arts doctoral program at the University of Minnesota. I also have been a lawyer and served as academic dean for a system of three schools in Minneapolis. Since my retirement, I have devoted much of my time to fiction writing. I am a member of the Loft Literary Center and draw much of my inspiration and motivation from the classes I have taken there. In the past two years I have become fascinated by the famous gay historical figures during the time of Shakespeare—including Christopher Marlowe, King James the First of England, and Francis Bacon. I have been writing a collection of short stories about them entitled* Queer Stories and Gay Adventures from Shakespeare's Time (For Fairies Only!).

JACK FRITSCHER, the founding editor-in-chief of *Drummer* magazine and its most frequent contributor (1975-1999), has been "romancing San Francisco" since the 1960s as the pioneer author of hundreds of stories and articles, photographer of a thousand published photographs, and screenwriter-director of two hundred videos. The author of twenty books, including *Gay San Francisco* (2008) and *Some Dance to Remember: A Memoir-Novel of San Francisco 1970-1982,* he is the surviving lover and biographer of photographer Robert Mapplethorpe, who he introduced to the San Francisco scene. He received the Erotic Authors Association Lifetime Achievement Award in 2007—his fiftieth year in publishing. Visit www.jackfritscher.com.

SHANNA GERMAIN is a poet by nature, a short-story writer by the skin of her teeth, and a novelist in training. Her work has appeared in places like *Absinthe Literary Review, Best Amer-*

ican Erotica 2007, Best Gay Bondage 2008, Best Gay Romance 2008, Best Lesbian Erotica 2008, The Mammoth Book of Best American Erotica Volume 7, and Salon. Visit her online at www. shannagermain.com.

MARK G. HARRIS was born during the Summer of Love in Greensboro, North Carolina, the site of the Woolworth's lunch counter sit-ins as well as the birthplace of O. Henry. His work is included in the romantic short-story anthology *Fool for Love: New Gay Fiction,* edited by Timothy J. Lambert and R. D. Cochrane (Cleis Press). Please visit www.markgharris. livejournal.com.

T. HITMAN is the pen name of a full-time professional writer who lives with his two husbands—the human one and his mysterious, otherworldy muse—in a small cottage somewhere in the wilds of New England. In their home, much romance is made, both on the page and in the bedroom.

DAVID HOLLY, as a bicyclist, has had frequent close calls with city buses, but he has yet to end up in Gay Heaven. His stories have been printed in gay erotic magazines and anthologies. Readers will find some stories and a complete bibliography at http://www.gaywriter.org.

LEE HOUCK was born in Chattanooga, TN and now lives in Queens, NY. His writing appears in several queer anthologies in the U.S. and Australia, and his other work includes poetry, pieces for theater, and art installations. Additionally, he has worked with Jennifer Miller's Circus AMOK! for many, many seasons. You can reach him at www.LeeHouck.com.

THOMAS KEARNES's fiction has appeared online in Blithe House Quarterly, Velvet Mafia, Clean Sheets, Night Train, The Pedestal, SmokeLong Quarterly, 3 AM Magazine, Word Riot, and Underground Voices, and in print in *Harrington Gay Men's Literary Quarterly*. An atheist and an Eagle Scout, he lives in East Texas.

JAY MANDAL is from southern England. After grammar school, he joined a City bank and worked in Europe. He has written three novels—*The Dandelion Clock, Precipice*, and *All About Sex*—and more than two hundred short stories, some of which are collected in *A Different Kind of Love, The Loss of Innocence*, and *Slubberdegullion*. He also has written a collection of one hundred flash fiction pieces.

NEIL PLAKCY is the author of *Mahu, Mahu Surfer*, and *Mahu Fire*, mysteries set in Hawaii. He is coeditor of *Paws & Reflect: A Special Bond Between Man and Dog* and editor of *Hard Hats*. A journalist, book reviewer, and college professor, he is also a frequent contributor to gay anthologies.

ROB ROSEN is the author of *Sparkle: The Queerest Book You'll Ever Love* and the forthcoming *Divas Las Vegas* and has contributed to date to more than fifty anthologies, most notably the Cleis Press collections: *Truckers, Best Gay Romance* (2007 & 2008), *Hard Hats, Backdraft, Surfer Boys*, and *Bears*. His erotica is often found in *Men* and *Freshmen* magazines. Please email him at robrosen@therobrosen.com or visit him at www.therobrosen.com.

SIMON SHEPPARD is editor of the Lammy Award–winning *Homosex: Sixty Years of Gay Erotica* and *Leathermen,* and the author of *In Deep: Erotic Stories*; *Kinkorama: Dispatches from the Front Lines of Perversion*; *Sex Parties 101*; and *Hotter Than Hell and Other Stories.* His work also appears in more than two-hundred-fifty anthologies, including many editions of *The Best American Erotica* and *Best Gay Erotica.* He writes the syndicated column "Sex Talk" and the online serial "The Dirty Boys Club" and hangs out romantically at www.simonsheppard.com.

J. M. SNYDER writes gay erotic/romantic fiction, has self-published several books in the genre, and has begun to e-publish through Aspen Mountain, Amber Quill, and Torquere Presses. Snyder's short fiction has appeared online at Ruthie's Club, Tit-Elation, Eros Monthly, and Amazon Shorts, as well as in anthologies released by Aspen Mountain Press, Cleis Press, and Alyson Books. For book excerpts, free fiction, and purchasing information, please visit http://jmsnyder.net.

NATTY SOLTESZ has had stories published in *Best Gay Erotica 2009*, *Ultimate Gay Erotica 2008*, and *Best Gay Romance 2008.* He regularly publishes fiction in the magazines *Freshmen*, *Mandate*, and *Handjobs* and is a faithful contributor to the Nifty Erotic Stories Archive. He is currently at work on his first novel, *Backwoods*, from which "Adult" is an excerpt. He lives in Pittsburgh with his lover. Check out his website: http://www.bacteriaburger.com.

SAM SOMMER is the author of *Bed & Breakfast*, a gay comedy presented in 2008 as part of the NY Fresh Fruit Festival; *'Til Death Do Us Part*, One-Act Plays that premiered on Theater Row, NYC in 1997; and *Attic*, at the Wings Theatre, NYC in 2000. His short stories have been published in numerous anthologies over the years, most recently in *Quickies III*, short fiction on gay male desire. His Off-Broadway directing credits include: *After Dark* (1998), *Attic* (2000), and *Summerland* (2001), published in *Plays and Playwrights 2001—the Best of the Off-Off Broadway Season*. He is the recipient of two Off-Off Broadway Review awards for scenic design, for *Cowboys* and *Tango Masculino*.

ANDREW WARBURTON is a PhD student specializing in literary theory. Until recently he worked as a copywriter, research assistant, and reporter in London, but moved to the United States to continue his studies. His fiction appears in *Hustlers: Erotic Stories of Sex for Hire*, *Best Gay Bondage Erotica*, and *Boys in Heat*, and his poetry has been published in the queer literary journal *Chroma*.

ABOUT
THE EDITOR

RICHARD LABONTÉ lives on a romantic island off the coast of British Columbia with his romantic husband Asa and their romantic dogs Zak and Tiger-Lily. He reads many books and writes about them; reads many, many short stories and edits them into such anthologies as *Bears, Daddies, Boys in Heat, Hot Gay Erotica, Where the Boys Are, Best Gay Bondage Erotica, Best Gay Romance 2008, Country Boys, Boy Crazy,* and the *Best Gay Erotica* series; and with Lawrence Schimel has edited *The Future Is Queer* and *First Person Queer,* winner of the 2007 Lambda Literary Anthology Award. Contact: tattyhill@gmail.com.